Gabriel Gaté – Internationally celebrated French Chef, Author and TV presenter.

***The Chef Who Made Onions Cry won my heart with the grumpy but loveable haute cuisine French Chef Armand and his pet pig. I laughed out loud I was so amused by the eccentric characters outdoing each other in the most surprising ways. It took me only a few pages to envelop me in this hilarious world.

Helen Lederer – British Actress, comedy novelist and award winning comedian and founder of *The Comedy Women In Print Prize UK (CWIP)*. Internationally known for her role in the comedy series *Absolutely Fabulous* and the BBC sketch show *Naked Video*.

***Very Very Funny –

Selena Summers – Journalist, Author (*Feng Shui In Five Minutes*).

***This is truly a comic masterpiece. There is a laugh on every page. As in her previous novel the plot twists and turns in Ms. Kippen's hilarious and deliberately absurd trademark style as she delivers another powerful social message.

Partick Edgeworth – Stage and Screenwriter.

***More wit and wisdom from a seriously funny writer.

The Chef who Made Onions Cry

A Goldfarb Adventure

By
Chilli Kippen

illustration: Aylie McDowall
Photo image: Cindy Karp.

Matador
9 Priory Business Park,
Wistow Road, Kibworth Beauchamp,
Leicestershire. LE8 0RX
Tel: 0116 279 2299
Email: books@troubador.co.uk
Web: www.troubador.co.uk/matador
Twitter: @matadorbooks

ISBN 978 1838594 077

British Library Cataloguing in Publication Data.
A catalogue record for this book is available from the British Library.

Typeset in 12pt Adobe Garamond Pro by Troubador Publishing Ltd, Leicester, UK

Matador is an imprint of Troubador Publishing Ltd

Contents

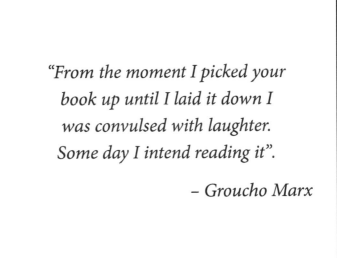

"From the moment I picked your book up until I laid it down I was convulsed with laughter. Some day I intend reading it".

– Groucho Marx

1

The Din

Master Chef Armand Barrique – twice Michelin starred – dreamt recipes. And always the best of his recipes came to him in the very early morning. Had Armand not dreamt of a unique way with truffle soufflé before he woke on the day he was due back at sea, had that extraordinary recipe for truffle soufflé not contained a new and wonderful ingredient, then the disaster may never have occurred.

In his haste to bake the soufflé and slide it from his oven to inspect it – to savour it – he completely forgot about sunrise. Had he stopped for an instant to inspect the sky and perceive the waking dawn he would have put a halt to proceedings and waited. But because this was his last day on land before he took to sea, and his last day with his beloved truffle orchard, his hens and his oak trees and his very precious truffle pig his inattentiveness to time could be forgiven.

As he opened the oven door and inhaled the delicate musky scent of truffle and the faint sulphuric smell of farm-fresh eggs, as he placed the gently pulsing quivering vision of perfection on the scrubbed pine table, Chef Armand's precious soufflé sank gently into a flattened sticky mess, blasted into submission by an ear-shattering sound.

The cacophonous noise came from a crackling loudspeaker through which a wailing voice bleeped and hiccupped repeatedly in a call to prayer that when it abruptly stopped was followed by a hissing sound reminiscent of a never-ending toilet flush.

Armand waved his arms around as though to shoo the dreadful noise out of his kitchen, but it was too late. He watched with horror as his soufflé entered its death throes and collapsed as though shot by a sniper. A blob of sour cream, which the chef had eagerly added, clung to it like a mating manta ray. Chef Armand Barrique clutched his bald head in his hands and screamed, '*Merde!*'

This was the latest outrage in a long list of affronts linked to the chef's neighbour, the imam of a small run-down mosque on the outskirts of the village. Chef Armand hated the mosque and the mosque hated Chef Armand, but the imam particularly hated the chef's truffle pig

Chef Armand hated the mosque because its loudspeaker system made his life a living misery. Five times a day it shattered his silence. Armand was convinced that the noise was the reason his nephew Pierre, who house-sat for him when he went to sea, had refused to stay again this year to mind the animals but had moved to Japan, where Armand rightly assumed he was guaranteed not to be billeted anywhere near a mosque.

Pierre claimed he wanted to learn Japanese but Armand was sure Pierre had gone to escape the din.

The dawn demise of his experimental soufflé was akin to the proverbial straw that breaks a camel's back, and the event that determined Armand's next course of action.

Rather than leave his precious baby truffle pig in the care of a neighbour, he decided to sneak the animal on board ship.

It became evident how much the imam hated pigs when only last week he and Armand passed each other in the village.

Chef often walked his pig through the village on a leash. The villagers loved the tiny creature and would feed it treats. However, the swarthy Tunisian imam, a man of wide girth and thick beard, had held his pock-marked nose in a very deliberate fashion and mumbled in accented French that the chef smelt worse than his pig and that someone – *did Armand imagine he heard the word 'Allah'* – should get rid of them both.

The comment naturally made the chef particularly uneasy about leaving his little pig behind. As a trainee expert truffle-hunter she was invaluable to him. It was with some self-satisfaction that he had re-named his pig Arafat, even though she was a sow.

His soufflé's untimely demise made up his mind. He would not leave Arafat anywhere near this imam. No imam would harm his pig. Off to sea with Armand his truffle pig would go.

On this, his last day ashore for several months, Armand lined a very large hamper with a blanket, tied a chequered neckerchief around Arafat's neck and lured the pig into the basket with a dog biscuit.

His ship, the *Pacific Belle,* was waiting in the harbour in Marseilles. He would take his chances with the captain, a Swede who preferred his fish pickled to properly prepared. Bad luck if the captain objected to having a pet pig on board. What five-star cruise ship could do without a *French* Michelin-starred chef? Not German or Swiss, but *French*. A five-star cruise ship without a Michelin-starred chef would be like a ship without a rudder, or a Peter without a Pan.

Chef Armand preferred to think that the odds were stacked in his favour.

2

Goldfarb

A day earlier, in another harbour a hundred and twenty-four nautical miles away, Pushkin Goldfarb stood in Japanese kimono and dark glasses, legs apart, arms akimbo and watched from his balcony as, below him, crew scuttled like ants up the gangway and on to the glistening white cruise ship the *Pacific Belle*. In their bedroom off the balcony, Brenda Willing, the love of Goldfarb's life, lay gently snoring, her red hair spread across the pillow like Medusa's and her ears encased in a pair of fluffy pink earmuffs.

Goldfarb hated the idea of cruising without Brenda. They had not spent a night apart since they met twelve months earlier on board the ship now berthed in the dock below, but she at least could sleep through noise, whereas he jumped at the sound of a feather dropping.

The cause of the noise that meant the nightly parting of the lovers was a pimply, unwashed heavy metal rock guitarist who called himself 'Skull' and lived in the next apartment.

Bertrand 'The Skull', lesser known as Bertrand Conard, happened to be the grandson of their landlady, a bandy-legged mega-rich French Lebanese widow. Madam Conard had kept her grandson's existence a secret until after Goldfarb had signed a two-year lease on his apartment. The Skull's stash of acoustic guitars, drum suites and grubby guitar players were part of the self-same secret. Mme Conard firmly believed that she had bred another Sting and failed to understand why other tenants in her building constantly complained. So keen was Goldfarb to sign a lease on an apartment close to a casino and overlooking the sea that he failed to read the fine print.

Madame sprayed a mix of croissant, apricot jam and Camembert at Goldfarb and Brenda over coffee in her office. 'Leave by all means,' she purred, 'but pay the entire two-year rental due until the lease expires.'

Goldfarb consulted with lawyers, but the lease was as unbreakable as a five-day-old bagel.

* * *

Brenda and Goldfarb had met in the casino on board the *Pacific Belle*, Goldfarb a professional gambler and

Brenda a compulsive but expert one. It was their love of gambling that drew them to one another and it was their love and skill at gambling that they hoped would offer them an escape from their sticky situation.

Brenda Willing, life partner of Pushkin Goldfarb, now asleep in their apartment in Monaco, ears blocked to the dreadful din of bass guitars by a housing of pink fluffy earmuffs, was the thirteenth wife of a Saudi sheikh before she met Goldfarb. She had been a sex worker in London when she received a call to serve a certain puce-lipped, oil-rich sheikh looking to be entertained in ways she knew best.

Now Brenda had pleased many and she knew the secret lay not in how she performed between the sheets but how they perceived her between their ears. *Find their fantasy, and you've got it made* were the words drummed into her by her first madam; and find and fill the fantasy was exactly what she did.

Acting on instinct, she arrived at the suite of the sheikh on the top floor of a swish London hotel wearing a burqa and looking like nearly every other woman on the top floor. When the sheikh opened the door, he was filled with wonder and a tremor of excitement. *Was this one of his wives?* He pondered. He thought he'd left them all at home.

Brenda quickly put him at his ease by showing her credentials and asking for her fee upfront, but when he asked her to take off the burqa, he was in for a surprise.

She would not let him see her face, or body. Twirling him so that his back was towards her, she gently but firmly put him across her knee and spanked him for a good twenty minutes, and then, before he could catch a glimpse of her ample breasts, she turned out the light.

Something extraordinary happened to the sheikh during this encounter. He took a nosedive into his favorite fantasy. So excited was he to make love to a woman of such purity, a woman who would not remove her burqa and expose her naked body even for him, that he made her an offer of a marriage arrangement on the spot.

Brenda was not the marrying kind, but a share of a sheikh's wealth was not to be sneezed at by a woman with a gambling habit, so she agreed to the arrangement on condition that she would never reveal her face or body to anyone but Allah. Faint with exhilaration, blinded by the sheer power of this fantasy, the sheikh bought her story holus-bolus and put the agreement in a binding contract the very next day.

Brenda smiled in her sleep as she replayed a re-occurring dream, of meeting the stranger in the ship's casino, the man with hair like a toilet brush who wore a Black Watch tartan dinner jacket, a casino tan and a ring on each finger. It was the softness of his eyes she found appealing.

That man was Pushkin Goldfarb, the man she now shared her life with.

Faced with the prospect of sleep deprivation they decided that Brenda, the sound sleeper, would stay put to play the tables at the casino while light sleeper Goldfarb took on the casino punters on their favourite cruise ship the *Pacific Belle*. In two weeks they hoped to make enough between them to buy out their lease.

And so it was that ship's chef and part-time truffle farmer Monsieur Armand Barrique and Pushkin Goldfarb, professional gambler late of New York City, were making their way towards the *Pacific Belle* – to make money and to escape noise.

3

The Albatross

The albatross was bored. He had followed the *Pacific Belle* on her world voyage and watched the endless flow of passengers boarding and departing. Now the ship had docked in Marseilles and people were boarding of all shapes sizes and colours in an array sufficient to confuse a fashion doyenne let alone a lone and elderly albatross. With his small black eyes, head cocked, he had observed the steady flow of baggage disappear into the belly of the ship like krill into the belly of a whale. A fortnight earlier baggage had spilt out again, was collected and disappeared. The albatross knew he was on to a good thing when it came to food and lodgings. Living off a ship's food waste was so much easier than diving for his own. Following a five-star cruise liner certainly had its advantages but it was the sameness of it all that had begun to pall.

Out of sight and out of sound the albatross could always find himself a nest of sorts and for exercise he would flap around the deck doing circuits, much like the passengers who braved the early morning breezes for what the albatross considered a rather silly way to spend the time for he, after all, had no option.

On this particular morning, hungering for diversity, the bird saw something unusual as he watched the passengers and crew come on board. His favourite chef, the French one with the head like an albatross egg and ears like clamshells, was back and boarding. The albatross had missed this chef, or more importantly he had missed his halibut in hollandaise. The albatross knew from years at sea that chefs burn out; the quality of their cooking suffers by the end of their term. But this was the beginning for this chef and the albatross looked forward to some delicious and exciting meals.

Something was different about this chef, who usually boarded with his egg shaped head lowered. Had he been blessed with vocabulary the bird may have described the chef as looking resolute, but the bird was just a bird. The chef was carrying a basket, the bird observed, and from inside the basket a small and twisted curly pink object corkscrewed out through a space in the wicker.

The bird was no Einstein but it knew that tails were usually attached to bodies so something must be inside the basket. From a replay of recent observations and a bird's eye view of the National Geographic channel through an open porthole the bird had learnt this tail had neither feathers nor hair and did not flick. What could it be?

In a flash, which to a bird's brain is a flicker, it came to him that there was a pig inside the basket. The albatross stabbed his beak at a mite in his wing feathers and reflected that there might be roast pork for dinner.

A day or so earlier, as passengers came on board, the bird set its sights on an image he had seen before. A small round figure draped in white sheets with only a nose and moustache visible and wearing sunglasses had climbed cautiously up the passengers' gangway followed by a second figure in a black tent and with no face visible. The bird was aware that on other occasions men wearing sheets such as this man did came on board followed by several figures in black tents but this entourage was confusing. The bird had an in-built inclination to besmirch any white covering whether it be on a chef, or a deckchair or even on a captain, so it was with some malice that he took flight and briefly hovered long enough to dispatch a green and slimy blob. It was a direct hit on the bump at the top of the sheet. If the figure in the black tent behind the sheikh in a sheet noticed anything at all it chose to ignore it.

Sheikh Hasim usually travelled with two of his wives but for this cruise he needed quiet. The past twelve months had been fraught with problems. The richer one got the bigger became one's problems. The older he got the harder he found managing his multiple spouses. Their bickering over trivialities was beginning to get him down.

Long ago the sheikh had worked out that life was far from fair and he found no rational reason to try to make it so. If he preferred one wife to another on any given day it was much like mixing up his breakfast cereal. Would anyone with options choose porridge every day if they could have cornflakes?

As a child with a multitude of brothers he became well versed in the art of elbowing, kicking and scheming to get his own way. He used these lessons from childhood to provide him with answers in later life. Many times as a child, his rambunctious siblings and their aggressive black-garmented mothers had beaten him to the ice-cream bar or the biscuit barrel. He was a small child, the runt of the litter, and his mother slightly overweight and lumbering, so it was not his fate to scramble to the front of the line to get the prime pickings.

This situation had planted in Sheikh Hasim the seeds of cunning and an uncanny ability to sum up his opposition with an element of objectivity. Two of his current wives, each appealing in their way, were engaged in warfare over his attentions. He knew they loved cruising so the ultimate penalty would be to leave them behind. Moreover, it left him free to philander with a decadent western woman, non-obbligato, and he was sure he would find one on board.

For this voyage he had chosen a new companion. One who was always on call and who didn't demand naps, shopping stops, black credit cards or prayer mats.

4

All Aboard

The sighs of passengers as they loosened their bras, slipped out of their shoes or dashed to the toilet blended with the sighs and creaks of the *Pacific Belle* as it tested its holding ropes against the tide. And as they reached for a glass of the bubbly, the sugar coated heavily accented Swedish voice of Captain Svensen oozed out at them from a loudspeaker system, welcoming them onboard.

Below, in the bowels of the *Pacific Belle*, Chef Armand Barrique looked around his airless, lightless cabin alongside the galley, his home for the following months, gently lifted his truffle pig Arafat from its basket, filled a tray with cat litter and wood shavings and vowed that after this trip his life would change.

He had for many years believed that one day he would turn his truffle orchard into an Air bnb, cook for his own pleasure and breed truffle pigs. But, as is the fate of many dreams, it drowned in a sea of compromise. His life had been spent instead catering to the quirks and qualms of others. His teacher, the great saucier Claude of Paris, would turn in his grave if he knew how many of his exquisite sauces Armand had diluted for the idiots who travelled on cruise ships. They sat at his tables smug-faced and precious and demanded a sauce with no cream, or no garlic, no lactose, no salt or whatever other food fetish they followed. He was drowning, Armand concluded, in a sea of ignorance driven by a school of greedy gastroenterologists, gerontologists and other 'ologists,' not to mention food gurus who made their living by advising neurotic patients how to eat less and eliminate more.

'*Merde*, they want to live longer and enjoy life less,' he concluded.

He, Armand, who worshipped the art of cuisine, had waded through this self-interested quagmire long enough and now it had to stop.

As he floated on this tide of misgivings he slid an envelope embossed with the crest of the shipping line from a folder attached to the door. It was addressed to him and contained a closely typewritten memorandum from the shipping line. The theme of the cruise confronted him in bold face: This was to be a *WELLBEING CRUISE* and would "Chef be aware of the special dietary restrictions as listed below. GUEST LECTURERS from the fields of Nutrition and Spiritual medicine will be on board and available for consultation".

5

An Invitation

The grinding of the anchor accompanied the gentle movement of the *Pacific Belle* as it slid slowly out to sea. Behind it lay the glistening glass kaleidoscope of soaring apartment buildings around the horseshoe-shaped harbor of Monaco, the masts of a thousand ocean-going yachts swayed like a bamboo forest, weirdly whistling in the wind.

The cruise around the coast had begun and shipboard life took over. The albatross that lived and fed off the ship tucked its small grey head under its wing and settled in, high on A deck, secure in knowing and bored by the knowledge that this cruise would be no different from the one before or the one that came after...or so the albatross thought.

Shortly after Goldfarb came on board he saw an envelope appear under his cabin door. He shuddered to see it contained an invitation; Goldfarb was a shy man who disliked attention, and for good reason.

His mother, Minchal Goldfarb, had made it her life's work to propel him into the limelight. A woman of humble beginnings and steel-like determination, Minchal had dreamed from an early age of one day producing progeny as great and talented as her hero, the writer Alexander Pushkin.

Although Minchal knew more about farming potatoes than writing poetry – she was the daughter of a farmer from Minsk – she nevertheless had her heart set on lifting her leg against the gatepost of fame. Armed with a few rubles, she arrived at Ellis Island and spread her legs, searching for a man of letters. It was unclear which man of letters shot the fatal bullet that fathered Goldfarb, but the man who marched the miles alongside Minchal and paid the bills was a kosher butcher from Vilna named Simcha.

Unfortunately for Minchal, Alexander Pushkin Goldfarb showed a lack of literary talent from a very early age. Beside herself with grief, Minchal turned her sights to Carnegie Hall and arranged for Goldfarb to take piano lessons with an alcoholic bookie named O'Leary. Convinced that the threat of anonymity was now lifted from her shoulders, Minchal proceeded to have two more children, sired by Simcha the kosher butcher, who went on, unaided, to win the Pulitzer and the Nobel prizes.

Goldfarb learned more from O'Leary than how to play Rachmaninoff or Chopin. He learned poker and blackjack, and through O'Leary he discovered the world that freed him forever from limelight or sunlight. Goldfarb discovered casinos.

Minchal had met her maker long ago but, like all good Jewish mothers, she lingered on in her son's head as an echo, a prodding finger, a reminder of what he could have been. And so as Goldfarb reached for the phone to politely refuse the dinner invitation a prod in his ear from his mother stopped him in his tracks. Her Eastern European voice rasped from the depths of his subconscious, 'Putz! You don't refuse an invitation to the captain's cocktail party or his table.'

The captain, a Swede, made a habit of inviting return guests to his table on the first night of a cruise. He had navigated the *Pacific Belle* for a decade and he knew her every creak and cranny. She was his mistress and he her master. He left no wife ashore, no family to return to. And of all the other loves in his life that came and went none were comparable to her. His one hope at the outset of every cruise was for peace and quiet.

Traditionally on cruise ships things happen. Older passengers die. On his previous cruise an elderly gentleman from Baltimore died while having a massage. The passenger, an octogenarian, continued the voyage in the ship's refrigerator. He was frozen solid and when he reached his point of disembarkation he could not fit into a wheelchair and his family had to wheel him away on a gurney. This was highly distressing for the remaining passengers and Captain Svensen spent a day on tranquilisers followed by an hour in the ship's sauna.

This was mild compared to an event twelve months earlier when a band of Somali pirates crept on board. With the help of a disloyal cabin butler, a Filipino named Peppe Gonzales, they took a number of passengers hostage on a neighbouring island. To add insult to injury the pirates used the ship's lifeboat to transport the hostages. Fortunately, their demands for money went unheard because the ship's wireless operator happened to be in bed with his lover at the time.

The hostages and a pirate who in the heat of the moment fell in love with a passenger, an African American from the South, were returned to the ship unharmed after the Manila police chief was alerted to the plot. The ship's butler, Gonzales, was detained and to the best of Captain Svensen's knowledge was still holed up in a cell in a Manila prison.

This changing world had certainly had an impact on Captain Svensen and of late his thoughts had turned to retirement and the benefits of a small cottage in Uppsala. Competition between cruise lines had ramped up and the advent of themed cruises meant more administration and staff training. The Learn to Salsa cruise almost caused a revolution with several passengers seeking divorce and others needing medical attention. Music recital cruises called for better sound equipment that could be adjusted to the latest thing in hearing aids.

He sensed that this latest Wellbeing Cruise would bring all hell to bear with his galley staff. An Indian yogic dietician and a spiritual master from Big Sur were the last people he needed meddling in the galley. He made a mental note to speak to the chef and the *maître'd* to pre-empt ruffled feathers.

As he fancifully mused on the changing face of cruising, Captain Svensen tweaked the dickey of his white dress uniform, patted on cologne and prepared to face the music. The traditional captain's cocktail party was about to begin. It was way past five o'clock and the sun well over the yardarm. The time had come to fortify with a tumbler of vodka and some caviar. He was no fan of the Russians but he savored their Beluga.

As he strode down the corridor, his whites flapping against his long lean legs, he mouthed a silent prayer to Aegir, the Norse god of the sea, for a peaceful and uneventful cruise. And Aegir the Norse god of the sea nudged his wife/sister Ran and smothered a smile.

6

The Captain's Table

A row of waiters stood at the ready like a row of Emperor Penguins, white cloths draped over black clad arms. The *maître d'*, pen poised, ticked off the name of each passenger and ordered a waiter to escort Goldfarb to the captain's table; ahead a Saudi sheikh and his black clad wife, arms linked with those of a short dark waiter's, were headed in the same direction.

At the captain's table, the Saudi reclined, like a pile of freshly washed laundry next to Captain Svensen, and his heavily veiled companion took the seat beside him. Goldfarb adjusted his dark glasses and sat down opposite. To the captain's starboard side was a stocky woman severely dressed but not unattractive with shoulders of a weightlifter. Goldfarb could almost hear his beloved Brenda whisper in his ear – ' this is not a good look. Shoulder pads are unfashionable.'

She seemed to Goldfarb to be a woman who wore clothes as though a uniform was a way of life. No ornament of any kind, no brooch on her severe jacket, no earrings to soften her hairdo uplifted her severe landscape. Goldfarb made note of her freckles and snub nose and marked her down as having Nordic origins. It was when Goldfarb took a hard look at the sheikh seated beside the captain that he did a double take. The sheikh nodded politely to Goldfarb, but no sign of recognition registered in his eyes. Goldfarb blinked. It was Sheikh Hasim, without a doubt, Sheikh Hasim, who had lost a fortune at blackjack to Goldfarb on board this very ship twelve months earlier; who had been taken hostage along with Goldfarb on that particular voyage from this very ship, Sheikh Hasim the former husband of Goldfarb's Brenda.

Goldfarb would never forget that acne'd nose, that warty mole, those puce lips, that face. It was indeed the same Sheikh Hasim.

Goldfarb felt a sharp stab of wounded pride. Was he, Goldfarb so forgettable? Had he changed that much in only twelve months? He metaphorically removed his deflated ego and examined it. It lay like a wrinkled balloon in the palm of his hand, shrivelled and wounded. He knew his hair was thinning – but the sheikh had lost a packet to Goldfarb in the ship's casino; was that so easy to forget? The sheikh looked right through Goldfarb as though he were invisible. Maybe, Goldfarb hesitated to assume, the sheikh was losing his marbles!

Goldfarb adjusted his dark glasses and driven by some childhood urge to get attention blurted out the question, 'Have you cruised on this ship before?'

The sheikh, a look of bored indifference fixed like superglue to his swarthy countenance, shook his head to the negative. Then, as suddenly as if bitten by a wasp, he leapt up, sat down and leapt to his feet again before plopping down on to his chair rubbing his backside. The black-clad woman leaned over and whispered in his ear. The sheikh's eyes popped open and like an automaton he bleated jerkily, 'Yes, I have been on this ship before.'

This jerky and confusing response surprised Goldfarb. Perhaps he had been right about the sheikh's behavior. Could it perhaps be St. Vitas Dance? As Goldfarb pondered on a new approach the rasping voice of his mother sounded in his ear. 'Leave it alone, you putz; better he doesn't know who you are. You're here to win money at blackjack remember?' and like every obedient Jewish boy, he listened.

The sheikh, head lowered, sipped hungrily on a mineral water but Goldfarb was very much aware of the woman's piercing black eyes glaring at him through the slits of the black burqa.

Goldfarb's reverie was interrupted by a tall very blonde woman of an indeterminate age, a woman who,

Goldfarb observed, was no spring chicken. The woman appeared to be all red mouth and large diamonds and smiled perpetually, even when speaking. She reminded Goldfarb of a TV newsreader. The blonde exhibited a set of even and blindingly white teeth. A little imagination shifted Goldfarb to the airwaves of his absent lover Brenda who, Goldfarb could almost hear remark, 'She should be wearing size 14 not size 10.' Brenda noticed these things about other women and like most men Goldfarb was susceptible to suggestion.

The blonde drawled in a southern accent, 'Y'all don't get up, let me introduce myself, I am Mrs Lawson-Groves of the Chicken Frizzle Fry chain in the United States and I am seeking comfort on board this lovely ship.'

Nodding to the captain she continued, 'Thank you for inviting me to your table Captain Svensen.'

Thus said, Mrs Lawson-Groves hitched her skirt a little higher, heaved life into her bulging breasts and sat down beside Goldfarb to whom she observed, 'We are the biggest fast food chain in the US of A.' She then wiggled a red-lacquered talon at Sheikh Hasim, and brayed, 'And we are about to invade you guys in the Middle East.'

There was a moment of complete and awkward silence as all around the table digested the word 'invade.'

'… With our chicken frizzle fry fast food outlets,' she added, and a sigh of great relief was heard from her table companions.

The sheikh's face fractured into a smile. His companion aimed her black stare directly at the blonde, leaned close to the sheikh and mumbled something. The sheikh blinked twice and bleated weakly, 'We run the biggest shawarma chain in the United Arab Emirates, so I don't think you stand a chance.'

The figure in black alongside him glared out at the table triumphantly.

'Shawarma? That's made from lamb isn't it and we call it kebabs,' the short, broad-shouldered woman innocently enquired. She then, wide-eyed, introduced herself to the sheikh, his companion and everyone in general as, 'Major Barbara Cock, retired US army medical corps and psychiatry unit.'

Goldfarb made note he was right about the uniform.

A dapper man, a floral silk cravat circumventing a remarkably thick neck, appeared at the table. His hair was crimped and grey and to his shoulders. He wore an ankle length black overcoat over what appeared to be designer jeans. A tinted monocle attached to a cord nestled in his left eye socket giving him a sinister but bohemian look, rather like a veteran of the Nazi SS.

'Dirk von Klimt,' he introduced himself in an educated English that smacked of Oxford. 'I'm the on-board art lecturer and auctioneer of fine art.' He gave a nod towards the captain and with a swish of his coat tail deposited himself alongside Goldfarb.

The party broke into a babble broken by a flourish of linen as waiters converged upon the table, pens poised to take orders. Serving spoons striking a battery of *bains marie* beat out a drum roll as Chef Armand materialised, a *toque blanche* perched cockily on his bald head, held in place by his shell shaped ears. The captain raised a glass to toast his two times Michelin rated chef.

Given the floor, the chef addressed his eager audience, a fixed smile on his face.

'May I suggest the grilled zucchini and ham hock salad and a twice roasted then pulled roast pork with macadamia and truffle stuffing with blanched pear,' he recited in a voice as smooth as a *crème brûlée*. 'Or for lovers of fish, a sea perch poached in white wine and basted in a hollandaise truffle sauce.'

He ended his announcement with a flourish of a manicured hand, but the moment was flattened like a hammer to sirloin as from somewhere in the vicinity of the sheikh and his companion a voice boomed, 'We don't eat pig. We believe it to be a filthy animal. I am surprised they have it on the menu.'

The lecturer smothered a snigger in the tail of his Hermes cravat.

Mrs Lawson-Groves, a frown denting her pristine facescape as though a shadow had fallen across the moon, queried to one and all and chef in particular, 'Isn't this a wellbeing cruise with a lighter cuisine?

Does the sauce on the fish have garlic? Garlic makes me awfully bloated and is the hollandaise safe? I suffer from lactose intolerance. Maybe you could hold the sauce? Of course, I don't eat fried.'

Goldfarb considered her claim that she didn't eat fried as somewhat in conflict with her fried chicken outlets. He noted the Arctic chill that had hit the air, mainly around the chef, and refrained from mentioning his own misgivings about cholesterol levels.

Chef Armand swiveled on his sandshoes, drew in his stomach, turned a dangerous shade of red and the word *audacité* stuck to his tongue like a half-sucked lozenge.

'Perhaps Madam would like her fish just poached in hot water? He hissed.

Time stood still and in that moment the image of Arafat his darling truffle pig locked in a small airless cabin with nothing to eat but a vegetable gateau overwhelmed him. The sheikh's words echoed in his head. 'I don't eat pig, filthy animals.'

Chef Armand smiled feebly, mumbling under his breath, '*Va te fairé foutre*', which roughly translated to 'Kiss my arse' and hurried out of a dining room filled with anxious faces, brushing away waiters as they grasped at his sleeves to ask about the menu.

A short while later a waiter appeared clutching a huge pepper mill and hovered over Major Barbara Cock, retired US army psychiatrist. He said he had a message for her from the chef: 'Madam, I'm sorry but chef refuses to overdo lamb and asked me to tell Madam, "Eat pink or don't eat".'

To placate her he added, 'Chef served up your meal himself.'

As Barbara took a second look at the shape of the gravy on her plate her training as a psychiatrist kicked in. Instead of gravy she saw a Rorschach inkblot and it came to her in an instant: this chef was trouble.

As Barbara picked her way through her rare lamb chops she reflected on her feeling of unease. Taking a second look at the pattern on her plate of gravy she assumed that her anxiety was about the chef. As an expert at reading inkblot tests she knew whoever put the gravy on her chops was very disturbed indeed.

7

The Casino

Pushkin Goldfarb made his way to the ship's casino after a troublesome first night dinner to find the room as quiet as Harrods after the summer sales. The croupier, a cockney from East London sat alone at the blackjack table reading a Barbara Cartland romance. Casting a weary eye at Goldfarb's drumming fingers on the table ledge he shed some light on the situation. 'It's the fuckin bridge players, the ship's full of 'em.' The croupier was not known for his subtlety.

'They won't gamble, this lot will fall asleep after dinner,' he snorted. 'You'd think butter wouldn't melt in their mouths but try playing bridge with them, then look out. They'd cut each other's throats for a high score.' He chuckled. 'Some of those old geezers have waited a lifetime to give their old ladies what-for. It's gags off and gloves on! Strange game bridge , they say it keeps the blood circulating.'

He chuckled again and went back to his romance novel, happy to have a break from punters.

Goldfarb had not counted on this being a bridge cruise. He was about to head for the cocktail bar when a vision in white appeared in the doorway of the casino. Following the sheikh at a respectable distance was his black clad wife; the sheikh glanced around the casino. Goldfarb wondered if this survey of the casino's barren landscape would jog the sheikh's memory but fortunately for all concerned Sheikh Hasim remained seemingly unaware of his previous connection to Goldfarb. Any memory of their earlier meeting had long been deleted along with the sheikh's shady business dealings and his discarded women. He seemed to have forgotten that in this same casino on board this ship Goldfarb had taken him to the cleaners, stealing first his wife and then his money.

One year ago, almost to the day, Goldfarb, the sheikh and Brenda had turned their attention to blackjack. Brenda had beaten Goldfarb, the sheikh and the smug cockney dealer and that was the moment when Goldfarb fell in love.

Whereas Goldfarb had fallen in love, Sheikh Hasim had fallen in lust. He had dismounted the stool and circumvented the blackjack table, leaned in close to Brenda and flapped a wad of notes under her nose, totally unaware that the lovely lady in red, free of a burqa, was in fact one of his wives. Goldfarb remembered it in detail but apparently Sheikh Hasim did not.

The sheikh threw Goldfarb a vague Tom and Jerry smile and he and his wife took their seats at the blackjack table. Goldfarb did not waste a second in joining them. Then to Goldfarb's astonishment the sheikh withdrew and stood behind his black clad wife. She clicked her fingers and the sheikh produced several chips for her to play with. Goldfarb smothered his admiration for this feisty wife the sheikh had brought along. He smiled at her but she glared back at him with a less than friendly look.

What luck, Goldfarb observed with certain pleasure, that she was feeling hostile towards him because that would put her off her game. The dealer put down his romance novel and dealt, and Goldfarb was in for a shock, Goldfarb remembered the sheikh's gaming style as though it were yesterday.

The play of each blackjack player is like a fingerprint, no two are alike and the identical play of the woman in the burqa to the sheikh's presented Goldfarb with a conundrum. Goldfarb never forgot a card player's system, their style of betting, and their sense of play so he had no doubts that the woman in the black burqa played an identical game to Sheikh Hasim.

Goldfarb was the better gambler so dropped only a few chips but he sensed that something strange was going on. The woman spoke hardly a word to him and when he shook hands after the play she nearly broke his fingers.

Goldfarb needed time to figure things out and called the game to a halt. Much to his surprise it was the woman and not the sheikh who clutched him by his coat sleeve and in a deep husky voice demanded a rematch before journey's end.

*"I never forget a face
but in your case
I'll make an exception"*

– Groucho Marx

8

The Double of a Double

Sheikh Hasim removed the burqa and blew his nose. His mouth cracked into a grin as he thought of the trick he had played on Goldfarb in the casino. It took four rounds before the peasant in his tartan jacket and sneakers realised he was playing with an expert and not some stupid woman. The sheikh had not won much but at least he felt he came away on top.

A julienne of carrots and miscellaneous breadcrumbs dislodged from the black fabric and hit the carpet. Dressing as a wife was definitely not for him. Eating while wearing a burqa was also not for him. It was like wearing a chaff bag. The sheikh had always had a flair for the theatrical. By dressing up in uniforms he had overcome the difficulties of being son number one hundred and seven in a two hundred and twenty son family. By varying his uniforms, he found he could attract the attention of his father the old sheikh who often mistook this son as an important military adviser from another government and would actually grant him an audience.

It was when wearing a uniform that once belonged to Napoleon that the sheikh had won the affection of his wife, Evangeline, who had a fetish about men in uniform. Another reason he much preferred a heroic military costume to a burqa.

As he looked in his mirror the sheikh could see across the way through an open door the smaller reflection of someone who greatly resembled himself. The other him was struggling out of a white thawb and now stood in only underpants and singlet. Apart from better calves, the sheikh reluctantly admitted, and more hair around his nether regions the man reflected from the adjoining room was an absolute double of himself.

This was entirely understandable as on this voyage he was travelling with a double and not the usual double of a double. This was in response to a series of threatening notes received by the sheikh and a failed attempt to smash him flat with a large drying cabinet flung from a rooftop. He knew any one of a dozen objectors to his many business ventures could have been behind the attack but he had no idea who. He tended to leave all his business to his accountant and head of human rescources Habibi. He had read somewhere that

Saddam Hussein had in his time employed a series of doubles to confuse his enemies but for the time being he felt justified in employing only one.

The sheikh's double, the figure seen following close on his heels up the ship's gangway earlier that day dressed in a burqa, and who had observed the albatross deposit a slimy blob on the sheikh's white robe, was one Sebastian Oliver, recently of the United Arab Emirates and late of the UK. He may have had his nose sculpted, his hair dyed and his chin chiselled and put on ten kilos to look like Sheikh Hasim, but no way was he taking a dollop of bird shit for him. Never one for forward thinking he failed to assume that should someone be gunning for the sheikh it would be a bullet he would need to dodge and not bird droppings.

After two years playing Doctor Jim, a vet in the popular TV sitcom *Happy Valley*, the writers of the series had him gored to death by a bad-tempered bull. The single but many partnered actor and part-time ventriloquist, now unemployed, did not hesitate to answer an advertisement on the internet for an actor with basic Arabic willing to change his appearance permanently.

So Sheikh Hasim chose to travel with an out of work actor from Ealing named Sebastian, who spoke a pidgin Arabic picked up from delivering Uber Eats for kebab shops and who had readily changed his nose, chin and hair and put on ten kilos to get the job; a double who was always on call and didn't need toilet breaks, naps, shopping stops, black credit cards or prayer mats and who didn't mind posing as a missus when necessary.

* * *

Because of his eagerness to play dress ups and dupe the decadent westerners the sheikh had failed to adequately brief his double and thus the evening had not gone well. The foolish double simply did not have answers to the simplest of questions and seemed to live in his own world. Only by pinching him viciously could Sheikh Hasim bring him into line.

What the sheikh did not count on was meeting up with Goldfarb, the dishevelled New York gambler who had left the ship on the last voyage with a lot of the sheikh's loot. Of course the sheikh remembered him. Not only did Sheikh Hasim hate to lose at blackjack, but also he particularly hated to lose to professional gamblers from New York who happened to be Jewish. And even though the money he lost gambling was plankton in his oceans of gold Hasim was not the best of losers.

Travelling with a double was not proving easy. The sheikh realised he could easily blow his cover if those who were after him could tell them apart. As far as he could make out the only giveaway sign was the strawberry mark on the left cheek of his double's buttock, a large blotch in the shape of a strawberry under which were tattooed the words, 'lick don't chew.' There had been some discussion about having the tattooed words removed but nothing could be done about the birthmark. The sheikh, Sebastian and Mr Habibi, the sheikh's accountant and head of human resources, had agreed unanimously that the chances of anyone seeing Sebastian's buttock were pretty remote. An image of Sebastian's left buttock cheek remained in a secret file on Mr Habibi's computer, secure and unavailable to the world at large. This one distinguishing factor between the sheikh and his double remained locked away securely and out of the hands of any would-be assassin.

The first to discover that the sheikh had a double was Sanchez the cabin butler. Sanchez, a small bandy Filipino, discovered these secrets over two cups of morning tea. As was the duty of the butler to the suites, Sanchez buttoned up his tails jacket that hung dangerously close to the ground, wiped his nose on his sleeve and drove the tea trolley into the suite taking care not to make too much noise. He had carefully arranged the cups and arrangement of pastries on either side of a red rose.

Sanchez was no expert at romantic settings but this much he had learned about this suite, that although it consisted of two adjoining staterooms with a queen-sized bed in each it was usual for him to find couples sharing one bed. He had done the turndown during dinner the previous evening and left a chocolate on each of the pillows of one bed. He had watched the sheikh and his wife depart the suite for dinner and heard them return about midnight.

He was thus ill prepared for what he found on his first morning of serving the sheikh's party: there was a sheikh in each of the queen-sized beds with not a wife in sight.

This posed a problem for Sanchez. He clearly needed another trolley and a second rose to service the second occupied stateroom. He glanced with caution into the second stateroom to make sure his eyes had not failed him. It was true; his eyes had not deceived him. There on the pristine sheets, was Sheikh Hasim sleeping on his side in foetal fashion – and in the adjoining stateroom there he was again, sleeping on his back and softly blowing bubbles through puce lips.

Sanchez was a simple fellow with little imagination and a positive outlook so he figured this could well mean a double gratuity at the end of the trip and promptly fetched another tray with a second rose for the second stateroom and tiptoed out of the suite.

News travels fast on board a ship and if the passengers were not yet aware that the sheikh had a double the crew certainly were. And there was one passenger on board the *Pacific Belle* with a particular interest in the sheikh, retired Major Barbara Cock, late of the US army psychiatric corps.

During her years as an army psychiatrist she had seen much action and patched together many damaged men, many who, in her humble opinion, had done little to deserve it. She had seen good men die and bad men survive and unlike the proverbial rolling stone gathering no moss she had acquired a moral compass as far as justice was concerned. Being a soldier came with a licence to kill but identifying the enemy could sometimes be confusing. She would never see herself as anti the establishment and regarded the law as vital. However, the law could often fail the victim and at such times it seemed clearly undisputable that there was room for vigilantes.

She had always done her duty and faithfully followed orders, but it seemed to Major Barbara Cock, now retired, that other forms of justice were needed in the world. As one who had seen men kill for a paltry serviceman's wage, the deal for professional assassins was not to be sneezed at. She had agreed to take this cruise because it suited an assignment that suited Major Barbara's moral compass, her moral compass as a paid assassin.

Major Barbara replayed events of the recent past that had brought her to being seated at the captain's table on board the *Pacific Belle*. She saw herself beside a white sea-going yacht bobbing gently on its moorings and mounting steps up towards a stark white mansion at the top of a hill. She had been brought to an island not yet mapped and had followed a Filipino manservant up a stairway cut into the rocks bordered on each side by tropical gardens.

The house was built mainly of glass and white stone. Standing between the heavily ornate Balinese doors was a small man dressed in white, with a mop of white hair and beside him was what appeared to be a small pony which as she approached she realised was a huge grey Great Dane wearing a jewelled collar. The dog had a massive head and soft yellow eyes and a translucent thread of dribble dangled to its shoulder.

The man spoke in a soft European accent of indefinite origins, his manicured fingers caressing his lips as he spoke as though every word was a secret.

'We do not need names, but for purposes of communication call me Rufus.' He spat the R and slurred the S to make a hissing sound and turned to the dog. 'And this is my wife Sophie.'

Barbara managed to compose her face into a mask of indifference while thinking, 'This man is truly crazy, but I know his face.'

Sophie extended a paw and dripped slobber. Barbara took the paw and shook it, avoiding the saliva. At first Barbara assumed that a two-legged Mrs Rufus was hidden away in the architectural glass marvel behind them but she found to her surprise as she learned more of her client, that this was not the case.

She followed Mr Rufus and Sophie into a room containing scarcely any furniture other than two massive couches overlooking an outdoor patio with a 360-degree view of the ocean. Several huge paintings were displayed and backlit. All were portraits of large dogs, some in evening dress, some languishing on a chaise lounge.

'My dear departed,' Rufus explained.

The manservant entered carrying a tray of Manhattans, and placed the tray on a long, low glass table, handing first Barbara then Mr Rufus a glass and placing a shallow bowl in front of Sophie. All three cocktails appeared to contain the same ingredient, the mix of alcohol, and a floating flower.

Mrs Sophie Rufus did not stand on ceremony. With a loud slurp and no apparent reaction to the alcohol, Sophie wolfed down her cocktail before their glasses had even been raised.

Mr Rufus snapped his fingers and a second servant materialised with a folder, another finger click and the folder was placed in front of Barbara. Rufus explained himself, hands prayer fashion.

'I am no lover of people; they make a mess of things. I cannot reveal to you my real identity but be assured that I have found that by advising presidents, creating chaos, manipulating governments and scaremongering I have made my fortune. You could consider me one of the richest men in the world.' He paused, sipped his drink. 'Although I have bought and sold nations the one thing I am absolutely certain of is that the animals on our planet are getting a raw deal and overall are better than people. I was once married to a woman who bore me children and that taught me a great lesson about loyalty or lack of it.'

Another pause as he marshalled his thoughts.

'But dogs, now that is an entirely different matter. Dogs make better spouses. Believe me madam if you have not loved a dog you have not lived.' His face softened. 'Sophie and I have been together for ten years –and we love each other purely, as was the situation with my previous canine spouses. We have grown into a single unit, we think and feel the same way.'

Then to the astonishment of the major he lifted a well-fleshed leg and in yogic fashion he scratched behind his ear with a bare toe. Undaunted he continued while the major struggled to suppress any sign of surprise at her host's dog-like movements. His voice had become soft with emotion

'Love comes in many configurations. If I die tomorrow Sophie will inherit everything – and no one can contest this, because legally – on this island, which I own and have citizenship of – we are married.'

And, with the hint of a pant, Mr Rufus bent his head between his legs in a motion that promised an attempt to do the physically impossible.

In a voice muffled by his white linen trousers he said, 'you will see in the future that I am merely setting a precedent that others will follow. The revolution has already begun. It is time to think outside the square.'

He allowed Barbara no time to think of a response, even if she had one, which she hadn't. She thought him quite mad, but maintained a look of sympathy, He had been an adviser to a president whose name she tried to remember, hoping against hope he did not dislocate his neck before he had paid her a retainer.

Returning to the vertical he proceeded to explain the reason for their meeting. 'I mete out revenge and the revenge I seek is for my four-legged friends, the sheep. On the ship you are about to board is a man with no feeling for sheep, nor for any other four-legged creatures I would imagine, otherwise how could he condone transporting sheep live but packed into the hold of a cargo ship without green grass or blue sky, simply to appease the gastronomic requirements of a section of mankind hooked on their own brand of hocus pocus.'

He ended the sentence on an up note. So worked up was Mr Rufus on the subject of the live transport of sheep that his face had acquired a mild purple hue.

At a loss for something to say, Barbara asked the obvious as the sunlight reflected in the gems on Sophie's collar. 'Is that collar real?'

'You have heard of the Duchess of Windsor's jewels,' he replied and that said it all.

'Cartier,' she whispered.

'Of course,' he replied.

A cloud cast a shadow over his shining purple pinkish face as though he suddenly remembered something ghastly. He shuffled in his seat and pointed to the file on the table.

'Your target will be sailing on the *Pacific Belle* out of Marseilles. Do not get caught. I shall deny any knowledge of ever knowing you. Make it slow and preferably in a confined space. Suffocation maybe? I would like him to know that particular brand of suffering.'

Sophie let out a loud belch and slid to the floor with a sigh, one eye shut and the other staring woefully at Barbara. The alcohol had finally kicked in.

* * *

Barbara Cock was army through and through. Her daddy and his daddy before him had been army men. When Barbara announced to her ma and daddy in their little farmhouse on ten acres daddy had retired to after leaving Washington that she wanted to be a doctor, daddy smiled and didn't miss a beat.

'Why gal, it's the army medical corps for you,' and for Barbara, that was that.

From an early age she'd realised you didn't question rank. As the middle child of three, orders came down the line, regardless of gender. She was barely a year into medical school when she realised the ranks were full of victims busy following orders or, to put it mildly, masochists. Young and inexperienced as she was she knew the field of medicine she should study in the army and chose psychiatry.

Her name had proven to be her nemesis but when she quietly hinted to her daddy she was considering a name change by deed poll an icy calm had settled and there on the spot her daddy made her swear an oath to keep the family name of Cock even if she married.

'It will make a man of you my girl,' her daddy had advised.

And in a moment of rare intimacy, his face softened like a shadow falling over Mount Rushmore. In a voice tinged with self-suffering and a certain pride he confided in his baby girl.

'Why, gal, I have been called many things "baby-maker, baloney pony, beaver basher, cranny axe, bratwurst, cum gun" and even "custard launcher", and from that I learned that names could never harm me, and I stayed with Cock and I rose as Cock through the ranks to be the man I am today.'

And as he handed Barbara the worn old family bible he made her swear to hold on to Cock forever.

She even weathered a brief spell as Biggun hyphen Cock during a brief and hazardous marriage to Lance Biggun, an army close-combat instructor, a liaison from which she emerged a little poorer but with a black belt in Judo.

* * *

Later that morning Barbara began to realise that her shipboard assignment would not be as easy as she had first anticipated. She was navigating through the breakfast buffet when she stood on a white thawb and as she stepped aside to avoid falling over she trod on a second white garment. Looking up she found she had come face to face with her target, Sheikh Hasim, the man she was there to kill, pondering the buffet table. Beside him stood his double. There they were, twin entities at the buffet table loading their plates, their white robes fluttering in the gentle sea breezes. No wife in black was anywhere to be seen.

In her time Barbara had confronted many obstacles to success, and equally as many unusual situations and even though this was a rare conundrum she tackled it with her usual finesse. Was the sheikh's party a twosome or a threesome? Last night at dinner the woman had not spoken. Could it be? This would be easy for her to establish.

To attract the attention of the pair and get a better look she crooned '*salaam aleichem*' into the ear of one. In tandem they turned to reveal identical profiles, identical noses, lips, moustache, eyebrows, sunglasses, and mole.

'*Salaam,*' one answered.

This was a carbon copy job, she observed, and a very professional one. As a military person Barbara was aware that this phenomenon among the ultra-powerful of hiding behind a double was growing in popularity. It was a trend gaining momentum along with the spiralling demand for hired assassins. Out of work actors, retired members of the military, Chechnyan bandits and semi-retired members of the mafia with kids still at private schools found the money attractive and thus a thriving industry was born. But as much as Barbara knew of their existence this was her first assignment that involved a double. Never had she been called upon to assassinate a double or a double of a double or a double of a double of a double.

She chose a seat with a clear view of the pair of sheikhs and closely observed them eating. They both used their fork in their right hand. Their taste in food did not give them away as both ordered scrambled eggs with a grilled tomato. They both squirted ketchup on their scrambled eggs. Each wore identical gold signet rings on the little finger. Their teeth looked identical and when they finished eating they both reached for a toothpick. This was not going to be easy Barbara decided as she observed her targets idly picking their teeth.

Barbara finished her coffee and headed for her cabin. She had work to do. The folder given to her by the enigmatic dog lover Mr Rufus contained no mention of her target having a double. Nowhere in her brief was there an order to dispose of not one but two sheikhs. These circumstances dictated she needed more instruction. She had no trouble with the ethics of this assignment. It sat comfortably with her moral compass. She was no lover of sheep, and she loved a roast of lamb, but she could find no rationale for transporting sheep alive in hideous conditions on a long and cramped journey, often without food or water just to be slaughtered. You wouldn't do it to a person; you shouldn't do it to a sheep. As much as Major Barbara believed in very little she knew that good was good and evil was evil and cruelty to dumb creatures, both two-legged and four, fell under her definition of evil.

'Find me a way to tell them apart,' she demanded in her text to Mr Rufus. 'Or should I do them both?'

The reply was immediate. An image appeared on Barbara's iPhone of a left buttock cheek with a strawberry shaped birth mark above which was tattooed *lick don't chew* followed by the text *hacked from Habibi computer identifying feature for double, image attached.* A postscript informed her: *sent from my iPhone.*

Barbara took a moment to reflect. She had to identify the sheikh with the tattooed buttock. And that was not going to be easy.

* * *

On this first morning at sea Barbara proceeded with her work assignment while Chef Armand woke with the events of the previous evening foremost on his mind. And foremost in his dreams had been the woman with the teeth bleating on about wellness, from whence led the prospect of an Indian person wrapped in a sheet poking around his galley. In his dream he dealt the woman a blow to the head with a menu and feverishly penned new menus all including pork to irritate the sheikh as well as the Mahatma person.

The chef was not one to indulge in ruminating but of late his grandfather had been much on his mind. Chef was a patriot, his patriotism learned at the knobbled knee of his grandfather. His grandfather had lost an eye as a fighter in the Resistance and this missing eye was a constant reminder to all the family of the price he paid for France and of everything French. His grandfather had particularly loved French food and his love of the cuisine had influenced Armand to train as a chef. Long after the war was over and the streets of Paris were French once again his grandfather slept with his one good eye open, ever on the alert for aggressors – a habit both distressing and frightening for his long-suffering wife, Armand's grandmother.

Chef knew his grandfather would turn in his grave if he could see the shawarma/kebab bars mushrooming all around Marseilles. He would rise from the dead should he witness his beloved *cassoulet* or *coq au vin* being prepared fat free and salt free to suit a health obsessed society.

Fuck wellness... Fuck nouvelle! These words erupted like a trumpet call from a mountaintop, a declaration of war on the part of Chef Armand – and his truffle pig Arafat stirred on her blanket beside chef's bed.

No more compromising, he muttered. He may be on a ship filled with food neurotics who thought themselves sophisticates but that was just too bad. Raising a clenched fist above his head he repeated, like a mantra, 'Fuck lactose intolerance, fuck nouvelle, and fuck wellness.'

The captain's memo lay on his bedside table: 'Dr. Rbib Dji of Mumbai, author of *Find Your Path to Happiness Through Food* and new age cardiologist Simon Schmitz PhD of Big Sur California, USA author of *Eat Raw, Live Longer* and *Go Paleo. Cave Men Had Better Sex* will be available on board for book signings and private consultations (Fees apply).'

Chef took the memo with him into the bathroom and, in an act of extreme defiance, used it as toilet paper.

So it was that Chef Armand strode into the galley that very morning in the blackest of moods leading a small pink pig on a leash, and around the pig's neck was a neckerchief. The chef handed the leash to the galley *plongeur*, a pimply-faced dishwasher named Mahmoud.

'While I am chef de cuisine on this ship,' Armand announced to the white frocked, predominantly black and yellow faced congregation, 'the cuisine will remain *haute* and French. The *saucier* will prepare sauces, undiluted, strictly in the *haute cuisine* fashion. No *nouvelle cuisine*. No gluten free, no sugar free, no lactose free, definitely no Paleo, nothing organic. We shall concentrate on offal. Armand does not cater to health fanatics and food weirdoes. If they want to stay healthy, then let them stay home. And' – he directed this comment to the Asian *entremetier* – 'and definitely no fried insects of any kind.'

As an afterthought he added, 'No substitutes! Forget low fat. Ignore salt free. Lard, lard and more lard, full cream, full cream and more cream, butter, butter and more butter. Long live *le croissant* and *la brioche*. And all Caesar dressing must have anchovy.'

Forming a fist, he raised his hand above his head and declared, 'Fuck nouvelle.'

The black and yellow-faced congregation of *saucier, demi-chefs, pâtissier, entremetier* and *poissonnier* stared back at him, glumly. It was more the presence of a small pink pig in their kitchen that bothered them. Outbursts by the chef-de-cuisine were not infrequent and their spoken English was limited. Finally, to anyone still listening, Armand added, 'Now let's get started on the menus for the week – *Dégage!* 'And to the pimply Arab dishwasher he bellowed, 'Mahmoud, feed my pig.'

* * *

Mahmoud the dishwasher was twice chosen. Once by chef to mind his pig Arafat and also by his uncle on his father's side. Why Mahmoud's uncle showed the foresight to predict a fate so glorious for his brother's child was very much to do with pork. His uncle was the imam of a small and rundown mosque.

The imam, who had one wife and a team of rugged sons, was the boy's protector. His family, his wife and his children and his nephew Mahmoud, lived in a ramshackle building alongside the mosque, the very mosque in the village close to chef's truffle orchard. The imam breasted his own sons like a pack of cards so it came naturally for him to choose his nephew Mahmoud to go to sea and learn to be a cook.

'There is money in food these days,' the imam thundered and added, 'and while you are on board you can also become a martyr.'

To see the chef prancing around the village with a pig on a leash the imam took as a personal insult. When he heard from people in his village the pig was renamed Arafat it ignited a flame within. The flame was fanned even further when he realised the chef was protecting his pig by taking it to sea with him. It was okay for the imam to throw stones at infidels but heaven help anyone who threw them back.

Grasping his nephew Mahmoud by his bony shoulders he thundered the following fatwa, 'Get rid of the chef's pig. And for this blessing you can anticipate a glorious passage to paradise.'

In response to Mahmoud's questions 'how?' and 'why?' the imam stroked his beard and stated, 'because the pig is a filthy animal, and the chef is an infidel' and, 'Go to Google. Everything is on the net.'

Even though he suffered from the atrophy of a closed mind, Mahmoud's uncle, the imam, was well aware that an average sixteen-year-old dishwasher could easily be influenced so, to make sure that his nephew carried out the fatwa on the pig, he breathed a word into the ear of another congregant named Ahmed, who also happened to be a *sous chef* on the *Pacific Belle*.

'Watch Mahmoud, make sure he does away with the pig,' Mahmoud's uncle hissed, 'and a dozen virgins will be waiting for you in Paradise.'

So unbeknownst to executive chef Armand, pimply sixteen-year-old Mahmoud the dishwasher, who became the minder of a small pink pig named Arafat, was the nephew of chef's arch enemy the imam, who considered the chef as well as his animal to be filthy and untouchable.

Like many other facets of existence, this bears a touch of irony. The Arab boy from Marseilles named Mahmoud had all his life wanted a pet – a dog or a cat – of his own. But never would he have thought that his first and only pet would be a truffle pig living in the shadow of a fatwa.

It seemed to the boy that Allah had meant for him to have a pig but he felt conflicted by it. Conditioned by the imam and his family to think of pigs as filthy and untouchable, he found to his dismay that he was drawn to the little animal, that the soft pink ringed eyes of the piglet sent tingling sensations through his solar plexus. And it was even more disturbing for him to discover that the pig had feelings, that it could smile when happy and sulk and even cry when upset.

A treat from the kitchen would make the pig smile, a difficult question like 'What is your name?' would make it frown, and a cross word from chef could bring tears to the little piglet's pink eyes. Never had Mahmoud seen such a sensitive animal. Like any pet that relied upon a human for food Arafat immediately assumed that this boy should be closely watched and she turned her attention and affections entirely toward him.

As a breeder of truffle pigs, chef knew their reputation as filthy and dirty was completely unfounded. Like many other urban myths, the reputation of the pig had gathered moss, the sort of moss, chef figured, that no longer held water. Their meat may have been unhealthy to eat back when the world was a desert but with the advent of refrigerators this made no sense. The chef was by nature a libertarian who respected the rights of the individual but this prejudice against the pig was verging on ridiculous. Pigs made good pets for eccentric owners; the actor George Clooney was renowned for this. They did not shed hair and if bathed regularly did not smell and had the best nose for hunting truffles chef had ever seen. On the current *truffe noir* market this meant 1500 euros a kilo or even more for black truffle. The British used dogs to hunt deer and shoot pheasant for sport but his truffle pig did no harm to anyone and promised to help Chef Armand pay off the mortgage on his truffle orchard.

Even in his native French the word *cochon* had seriously negative connotations. As well as meaning pig the term *cochon* meant kinky, perverted, obscene, and consumer of all things nasty. This could hardly describe his truffle pig or any truffle pig that had come before her. To label these wonderfully clever creatures in such a way was in chef's mind a gross misdemeanor.

'I never worry about diets. The only carrots that interest me are the number you get in a diamond".

– Mae West

9

She Who Collects Houses

The next day, a day at sea, Goldfarb was heading to the barista to get a coffee when he passed an open door marked Supervised Bridge. In the room beyond he saw a group of men and women, most of them elderly, seated in sets of fours at small tables, waiting patiently as a buxom woman dressed in what appeared to be an old-fashioned public school uniform handed out packs of cards. Although it was mid-morning several of the card players appeared to be asleep. When the woman in the uniform rang a small bell the slumbering gents sprung to attention. Goldfarb slid through the door to watch.

He tried to follow the game play but found it quite confusing. Nothing much happened until a tiny mouse-like woman snarled much like a Jack Russell at the man opposite her who was playing the hand. A small outcry occurred and the tone of the game immediately altered. It went downhill from there as Goldfarb witnessed what one could only describe as a bloodbath. Hands reached up and a battle began to attract the attention of the woman in the uniform who was labelled with the title of Director.

Players snarled, glared, thumped tables and threw down cards while they waited for the director, being very much a peacekeeper, to reach their table. Pencils were broken. There was spitting and shrieking and foul language. One elderly gentleman, a Brazilian by his accent, yelled so hard in Portuguese that he spat out his teeth that the long-suffering director rescued off the floor.

Well into the play a meek gentleman was helped from the table with a bleeding shin. His wife, a larger woman with grey hair and a faint moustache, maintained a look of innocence but claimed her husband had lost the game for them by not bidding his hand.

'He won't bid a slam, he won't ask for aces, he's forgotten four no trumps,' she kept mumbling as her husband was helped to the ship's doctor.

Goldfarb felt he had witnessed a chapter of an unpublished book by Franz Kafka. But maybe, just maybe, this frenzy to win could be redirected – straight to the blackjack table? He was still pondering on this when Pamela Lawson-Groves appeared like an answer to a prayer and greeted him.

'Remember me from last night?' she crooned and a sculpted eyebrow rose.

* * *

Mrs Lawson-Groves III, Pamela to her friends, collected houses. From a very early age, when first she won a contest as a Beauty Belle, Pamela set her sights on marrying for houses. Growing up as she had in a Southern trailer park, she had never known a house. She lived in a motor home permanently parked beside a toilet block in a small town. In the summer it was hot, in winter they froze. When, as fate would have it, she became Beauty Belle for the county, media attention and her wonderful legs propelled her into the limelight.

As Pamela had little education except knowing how to read it seemed her lot in life was to become a trophy wife. As a trophy wife, she learned the importance of adapting. Husband number one, a devout Mormon with a mansion on the edge of Salt Lake City, a ski lodge and no other wives still living, liked his good lady to appear in modest garb. Pamela dressed modestly, wore her hair in a bonnet and sang in the tabernacle choir.

Her second husband, a Texan rancher with several thousand acres and a homestead, liked his gals to show a little leg so Pamela dressed accordingly and learned to lasso cattle when the need arose.

When Pamela finally hitched her wagon to Peter Lawson-Groves III, a senator in Washington, she saw the need to improve on her etiquette, dress like a senator's wife in elegant gowns with designer labels and learn to mix a good martini dry.

Senator Lawson-Groves III, who was not always totally upfront about his other interests, owned a fast food chain with a multi-million-dollar turnover. It was the fastest growing such chain in the United States and the senator kept several thousand chickens always on the ready. As further fate would have it, during an argument in the Senate about high hormone levels found in caged poultry, the senator clutched at his heart and dropped dead. Thus did Mrs Pamela Lawson-Groves III become the sole owner of their house on Washington Hill, a fast food chain with a turnover of close to a billion and a pending class action suit.

One thing Pamela could claim that was not an acquired affectation was the game of bridge. This brain-draining pastime was all the go in Washington and even back in Texas the local ladies loved to play a rubber. So Pamela Lawson-Groves III came aboard the *Pacific Belle* to cruise and play bridge and if it was so written in the stars, to acquire more houses, along with a husband.

It was no surprise that a man of early retirement age and seemingly alone attracted Pamela like a bee to honey.

'Y'all play the game of bridge?'

Goldfarb extracted his arm from Pamela's claw-like grip and responded, 'Well, I'm a blackjack man myself.'

Pamela glinted at him with a row of perfect teeth. 'Honey, I'm always willing to learn.'

And there, on the spot, straight out of left field, the question of how to solve his problems was answered.

'Then perhaps I'll give lessons. Are there other bridge players who may be interested?'

Goldfarb left the question dangling like a carrot in front of a donkey and like a donkey seeing a carrot Barbara took a bite.

'Why, sir, then I shall rally the troops.'

And there it was, as easy as taking candy from a baby.

Goldfarb excused himself and exited before another round of the bloodbath known as bridge was due to start.

> "*The Secret of Life is honesty and fair dealing. If you can fake that you've got it made*".
>
> – *Groucho Marx*

10

A Real Piece Of Work

Goldfarb meandered down the corridor to the ship's theatre where a lecture on art was due to start within the hour.

The theatre was empty except for his dinner companion of the previous evening, the lecturer von Klimt, shuffling through papers at a lectern. Goldfarb waved casually and went on his way. He had no interest at all in art.

Art was Dirk von Klimt's 'thing.' After a short career as an art critic, during which he cast afloat the career of several very average artists on a tide of hyperbole, he woke up to the reality that modern art, like fashion, came in trends, that the art collecting public are easily manipulated into hooking their investment wagon to any rising star if a dollar sign is blinking in the distance.

Dirk threw in his job as auctioneer with a leading auction house and headed for greener and richer pastures. He looked towards the third world where native artists worked for pennies and there he set up a factory committed to creating original moderns and copying modern originals. Several quick trips a year and Dirk could claim ownership to works by every modern painter hanging in the Met. To give that added touch of authenticity to his originals Dirk employed a copywriter by the hour to give them spin, a credible provenance and a bio of the artist. The art reporters who write the art-speak no one understands waited with open arms and empty pages for their next exclusive story.

He was born in New Jersey to Valda and Howard Shearling and named Albert (Bert for short). It was at the table of his aunt Sal and uncle Benny that he was taught that his uncle Benny was an artist, and one with a quite outstanding talent. The fifty-dollar note uncle Benny handed out to all the cousins for Christmas was all his own work; forged fifties were uncle Benny's artistic magnum opus.

When the police finally caught up with uncle Benny, his fifty-dollar notes went down in history as the finest they had seen and one remains on display in the National Crime Museum. It could thus be said that forgery was in the blood, and nested in young Bert's subconscious like an egg waiting to hatch. As Bert grew into his chosen profession of art dealer he became aware that to impress his target market of ill-advised, moneyed-up and very pretentious art collectors he needed to change his image to one that better met their expectations.

So Bert Shearling morphed into Dirk von Klimt, the A-list trend setting art expert, friend of rich widows and social and gossip columnists. One slightly used monocle from a Neo Nazi costume shop in the East village, an Armani coat that swept the floor and faded jeans with worn to the point of threadbare knees, hair extensions and, 'Voila!' exit Bert Shearling and enter Dirk von Klimt. With acting lessons from a drama coach to cultivate a voice like George Sanders his transformation was complete.

Much like Arafat, the chef's truffle pig that snuffles for truffles, Dirk could sniff out greed in vulnerable art collectors. Very early in his career as a manipulator of the art market Dirk realised that cruise ship passengers presented a sitting target. Money on five-star cruise ships was often not a problem, even though the money and its owners were not so easily parted. But of one thing Dirk was certain, investors in the art market had a nose for profit. That was not to say that genuine art lovers also cruised who would buy a painting because of its appeal, but Dirk's real target was the art investor out to make a profit, specifically those who would not know a work of art from a sow's ear.

In Monaco, where Dirk had taken up residence many moons ago, he learned that to a greedy investor any second-rate painting could be transformed into a major work of art through clever marketing tactics.

* * *

'The artist called this painting *Day*. He completed this astonishing piece just before he died and for years it has been languishing undiscovered in someone's attic. This artist has many paintings hanging in The Met.'

Dirk stood before a massive stark white canvas and scanned his audience for signs of reaction before again bombarding them with dense information.

'Look closely at this canvas and you will see tiny specks that represent the rising of dawn. This is typical of post modernism.' He glanced at a man in the front row and saw his eyes glaze over. Lighten up; he urged himself, you are losing them. A woman in pink with her hair in a net seated in the third row was waving at him frantically.

'But there's nothing to see, it's just a white canvas.'

Dirk resisted the desire to throw a piece of chalk at her as he remembered a teacher doing to him years ago in a classroom.

'Oh please, madam, just a white canvas! Would you describe Franz Kline's *Black White and Gray* as just a black, white and gray canvas? After my lecture

I shall have all the paintings you see here hung in the gallery. Then you will see for yourself the drip method the artist has used, the drip method with paint used by the great Jackson Pollack. Believe me, madam, this is a prize for any collector of modern art – but if you want something more definitive then perhaps...'

'But who painted it?' The same woman again, if he had a gun he would have shot her.

'The artist studied the techniques of the great Franz Kline. Franz Kline's paintings hang in the Met and all great galleries. But perhaps for madam, something more colourful?'

He clicked his fingers and two assistants heaved a huge colourful smudge on to a stand.

'This artist's work will one day be worth a fortune. He will be prized amongst collectors. Collectors who had the foresight to buy a Warhol in the nineteen fifties when Warhol was just a commercial artist are very wealthy people today. They took a gamble and it paid off. Collecting up-and-coming artists is a calculated gamble but with the help of a curator such as myself. Well ...that is why I am here. Should anyone wish to put together a collection, please take my card. I work internationally online.'

'So how much for this one if he's not well known yet?' There she was again!

'Madam,' Dirk purred his words in the fashion of the late George Sanders, 'we auction these pieces, but believe me whatever you pay for one you will consider as cheap in ten years' time.'

'So who is the artist?'

She could well be a potential collector even if she was extremely irritating. He handed an assistant a colour brochure with the picture of a blond young man painting in a studio that, judging by the background, must be somewhere on the Riviera and motioned him towards the woman.

'His name is Jacque D'Peppe, a name you should all remember.'

He addressed the wider audience of potential modern art collectors and bored passengers with nothing else to do with as much passion as his George Sanders impersonation would allow. If he sold one of Charlie's paintings the kid would be delighted and in his mind's eye he saw little native Charlie who lived with his mother in a village in Sumatra walking away with fifty US dollars and feeling like a millionaire.

But as the world is yin and yang so did Dirk von Klimt have vulnerabilities of his own. And his weakness was gambling. Dirk would bet on a race between two beetles. And like any gambler bitten by the bug, it came as no surprise to him to feel that familiar gut squeeze as he riffled through his lecture notes, the gut squeeze that was a symptom of the need for that adrenalin rush, the rush that he could only get from a good old-fashioned gamble.

11

Mutiny

As he sat alone in the dining room on this, his second night at sea, Goldfarb had misgivings. Earlier that evening the sheikh had passed Goldfarb's table accompanied by his double, the double dressed and looking identical.

Goldfarb realised instantly that he had been duped, that his suspicions about the state of play at the blackjack table had been correct. The woman playing that night had hardly spoken and had the grip of a sumo wrestler. There was no woman with the sheikh or, if there was, she was under wraps. While Goldfarb wondered if the sheikh and his double would try trickery again he felt a light tap on his shoulder and blinked up over his Roquefort cheese and Armagnac at the gleaming white teeth of Pamela Lawson-Groves III.

'May I?' She pulled up a chair without waiting for his answer. Goldfarb felt he knew what was coming.

'Would you care to instruct a few bridge players on the rudiments of blackjack, because I have a few volunteers eager to learn?'

Goldfarb felt he had been tossed a lifeline. Only too eager to oblige, he agreed that they meet at the casino after dinner. Pamela left to join another table and as Goldfarb contemplated a new and exciting source of income he became aware that his waiter had thumped his coffee down with more than usual vigour.

An earthquake in the galley had begun. Chef's declaration of war was rattling cages. It started out with a waiter asking for a hollandaise without butter and it went downhill from there. The waiters huddled in a cluster at the galley door, the small computers they used for taking orders dangling listlessly by their sides.

Their drooping shoulders and anxious expressions signalled their despair. It was obvious they didn't know what to do.

'No special requests, by order of executive chef,' Ahmed the *sous chef* bellowed without looking up. 'But what do I tell the passengers?' queried an anxious waiter. 'Don't ask me,' Ahmed replied.

After lights-out in the dining room, a union man, a Scot named Hamish, addressed a gathering of the kitchen staff.

'I think the chef has lost his marbles,' he pointed out. The Malay butcher began to search the floor for these marbles. Observing their blank looks and the Malay's upended backside Hamish chose his words more carefully.

'I think the chef is having a nervous breakdown. We should go to the captain and report this. We cannot go on ignoring special requests in the kitchen, the passengers will mutiny.'

'Yes, yes,' echoed the *sous chef* and the others grunted their agreement.

There was a general rumbling of approval amongst the English speakers, the remainder set to preparing the breakfast buffet.

12

Bridge Brigade

The casino was as quiet as King Tut's tomb. Goldfarb knew he needed to make the most of any new recruit who wanted to learn blackjack but felt a stab of conscience about taking money from the innocent. Rock music streaming from the dance club jogged his memory of why he was where he was on board and he felt a pang of desire for his beloved Brenda. He remembered what he had to do; he was on board to win enough to pay out their lease so that they could get a good night's sleep together.

The croupier dragged himself away from his Barbara Cartland romance and acknowledged Goldfarb but his expression changed from bored to bewildered as a crocodile of passengers led by a tall blonde headed for his table.

'Blimey,' he whispered under his breath, 'here comes the bridge brigade.'

Pamela Lawson-Groves strutted assuredly ahead of two ladies who, judging by their dresses, were in their early teens and a gentleman on a Zimmer frame who appeared from the position of his head to be semi-comatose. As they hit the overhead lights, the two girls in their teens morphed into very short, very thin, very old, very fashionable ladies with bows in their hair. They smiled at Goldfarb and the croupier and exposed teeth of a variety of shades of glaring white between red-rouged, rosebud-shaped lips. Goldfarb sensed he was about to enter a lion's den,

The two elderly teens introduced themselves as friends and widows Fanny and Ethel from San Francisco. With old world charm they thanked him for offering to teach them blackjack. As an afterthought, they politely enquired about his marital status. Goldfarb took note of the diamond rings on each finger and the massive amount of gold chain around each thin and rather scrawny neck.

The glint in their heavily fringed eyes was an indication that they were looking for trouble, and he hoped he was not the trouble they were looking for. Their concerns seemed to be about falling asleep but Goldfarb assured them that betting at tables would definitely keep them awake, as would the game of blackjack itself. Fanny revealed she was a retired dentist and Ethel, a retired litigation lawyer. Goldfarb found this to be a frightening discovery.

Maurice, the gentleman on the Zimmer frame, emerged from his trance, straightened up and lifted a gnarled hand at Goldfarb in greeting while he explained himself away as a retired accountant from the UK.

Previous lives accounted for, Goldfarb ushered them around the blackjack table to face the croupier who emerged from behind his novel with a bemused look on his face and ready for action.

'Don't underestimate, don't teach any good moves,' the voice of his late mother rasped in Goldfarb's ear. Goldfarb, who believed that any job was worth doing well, for once ignored her. As his eager students gathered around the table a scuffle ensued between Pamela and Ethel for the space alongside Goldfarb. Acting out the role of diligent teacher, Goldfarb began with the basic pointers of the game, which to his eager students appeared to be simple to the extreme. The aim was to get as close as possible to twenty-one points and not go beyond this number, he explained. The cards two through to ten were worth their face value and kings, queens and jacks were each worth ten. Aces could be counted as either one or eleven.

'The object for each player is to ask for cards totalling as close as possible to twenty-one while exceeding the hand held by the dealer or, in this case, the croupier,' said Goldfarb. 'The best total of all is a two-card twenty-one, a blackjack.'

He added that the dealer played with three packs of cards and that the device holding the cards was called a shoe. The shrunken Maurice, retired accountant from the UK, changed his glasses and leaned forward eagerly.

'How many packs?' he squeaked in a shaky voice.

'Three.'

The cockney croupier started to deal.

To Goldfarb's surprise his enthusiastic elderly students seem to pick up the game remarkably well and play soon began in earnest. Only Maurice the accountant held back and placed no chips on the table.

To quench any feelings of guilt he had about raking in their money Goldfarb focused on the bejewelled hands holding cards around the table. Combined, they could fill a Bond Street jeweller's window. Fortunately for Goldfarb, who was well ahead, the long day took a toll on Fanny and Ethel and they began to fade. With thankful glances at Goldfarb and Pamela they cut their losses and left the table with promises to continue the game the next night. Maurice, the retired accountant, sat immobile on the seat of his Zimmer frame, Goldfarb unsure if he was awake.

Not a bad night's work Goldfarb thought as he realised he could easily reach his target with this group of gambling bridge players.

'Can I help you back to your cabin,' Goldfarb asked Maurice, abandoned by his female companions like a discarded bag of refuse.

'Interesting game.' Maurice spoke for the second time in a tremulous voice. 'I'll come again.' Thus committed he lowered himself to the floor with the speed of a giant turtle and embraced his Zimmer frame. He headed for the casino door without a backward glance.

Goldfarb eagerly scooped up his winnings. The croupier offered to deal but Goldfarb resisted the temptation. 'Get out when you are ahead,' his mother rasped inside his head and this time he listened.

'Watch out for that lot,' the croupier warned, 'bridge is a numbers game too, and that lot hates to lose.'

* * *

However, Pamela Lawson Groves III had not yet kissed the day goodnight. After a lipstick stop at the powder room she returned to find only the croupier and a Saudi at the blackjack table. She sat down alongside the sheikh and cast some chips out on the table.

Only late at night did Sebastian dare to do 'the sheikh' act alone. Being convincing as a double called for him to improvise. This evening at the captain's table had been difficult and his ribs ached from being jabbed by Hasim's bony elbow. He needed a cigarette and a stiff Scotch and like anyone who lives cheek by jowl with another, he needed a break.

'Go, but be careful and keep your mouth shut,' the sheikh had cautioned. He, too, was secretly relieved to be free of Sebastian and his personal hygiene problem.

Sebastian felt secure as he mounted a stool and motioned the croupier to shuffle the cards. Only night owls prowled in ships' casinos, he assumed. So it came as a surprise when he got the first whiff of Chanel 5, the whiff of Pamela Lawson-Groves III. The house won two hands before Sebastian felt an intimate touch on his hand and swivelled to face a smile as blinding as an Elton John dinner jacket.

'I've never been to the Middle East, are you from Israel, that place full of Joowish people?' Pamela asked in little girl voice.

Peoples' naïveté when it came to other cultures never failed to surprise him. Even in multicultural Ealing his fellow countrymen, himself included, couldn't tell a Korean from a Japanese or a Chinese from a Tibetan and would not have a clue about their cultures. But never in the oceans of ignorance that he waded in had Sebastian encountered anyone who would think a Saudi sheikh would come from Israel. The earth felt firmer beneath his feet. 'No,' he responded, 'I am from Saudi Arabia.'

'Oh, you people have an airline, I've seen the commercial on TV.'

This woman is quite sheltered, he concluded with some kindness; or maybe it's an American thing. He felt even more secure. He saw her glimpse at his naked wedding finger and pre-empted her by asking, 'Are you married?'

She wore a dozen rings on her wedding finger and several diamonds, testament to previous marital alliances. She hung her head modestly and softly voiced, 'widowed' and, as any professional actor would do, he pretended sympathy by nodding and patting her hand.

'And you?' she countered.

He had learned from being a double that the easiest way to lie was to keep as close to the truth as possible and so he told the truth, 'Never married.'

She seemed surprised. 'And do you live alone?'

This was treading on dangerous ground. 'Well, no. I have a double to protect me when my life is under threat as I am a very wealthy man.'

'Under threat?' Her eyes widened to saucers. 'But at the captain's dinner you were with a woman.'

'My double dressed as my wife.' He felt it was time to change the subject.

'And you,' he asked politely, 'where do you call home?

She explained with utmost modesty that she had several homes, Salt Lake City, Dallas and Washington to identify just a few.

With the agility of a featherweight and the diplomacy of Ban Ki-Moon Sebastian segued the conversation to another level. From behind his hand in a manner of extreme secrecy he feigned distress and begged Pamela not to blow his cover by coming up to him in public when he was with his double, which could somehow give his game away. This, he explained, could identify him to his enemies and put his life at risk.

He then gallantly took her hand and kissed it. Gazing longingly into her eyes he asked if he could call her so that they could meet during his escape from his double and continue 'this delightful *tête-à-tête*.'

Mesmerised by his gallantry, Pamela squeaked an agreement along with her cabin number. The last thing he heard was, 'we both own fast food chains. We have so much in common.'

Sebastian wiped a drip of perspiration from under his nose with the cuff of his white robe. His first solo act without the sheikh had gone better than expected. An heiress with a fast food chain and good legs was not to be sneezed at.

13

Sanchez Mendez

Major Barbara Cock had six more days to identify her target. Six more days to find which sheikh had the tattoo on his backside. This was her only pathway. Find the tattoo and identify the double or do them both. Her employer, Mr Rufus, had mentioned suffocation as the preferred method, but that was before a double entered the picture. That left the sheikh with the pristine backside to somehow be tossed overboard. A jab through his white robe, a minute for the drug to take hold and Presto! She knew this would not be easy, it would be harder to identify the sheikh from the double than to toss him overboard. As she took a stroll around the deck she passed the sheikh and the double beside the pool sheltering under an umbrella reading.

Adopting a look of bored indifference, she strolled towards them. Pretending to trip, she bumped against the table and sent a book flying from the hand of one of the readers. The book fell on to the deck and opened to reveal a double-page spread of scantily dressed women with a passage of text in Arabic writing. This told her nothing about the reader.

She excused her clumsiness and handed the book back to its owner. Could he read Arabic or was he simply looking at the pictures? Neither sheikh seemed particularly pleased to see her and both slammed their books shut as she stood above them making inane comments about the weather. She noted that apart from their faces very little bare skin was visible as they sat tented in white under the umbrella. Catching a glimpse of a naked behind with these two would be as difficult as catching a glimpse of the US president on the toilet.

Thinking of the US president on the toilet gave her another idea. She nodded and they silently nodded back and she headed for A-deck where the five-star suites were located.

* * *

The five-star suites were considered VIP accommodations on board the *Pacific Belle*. Each suite was serviced by a butler and in the suite occupied by Sheikh Hasim's party Sanchez Mendez the Filipino butler was making up the beds. Barbara observed his inappropriate dress, the standard uniform for butlers on board the *Pacific Queen*, of grubby tails and dress shirt. *He looks like a cross between a poor relative at Eton and a flasher at Ascot,* she mused.

Sanchez was methodically creasing a corner of the sheets when a short, blunt woman in khaki shirt and shorts poked her head warily around the door of the suite. Major Barbara Cock smiled broadly at him and said her name and cabin number by way of introduction.

Sanchez was a simple soul with a wife and six children to support who sat squarely at the bottom of the food chain and well he knew it. He therefore listened when this short and very plain western passenger asked him for a favour. When she slipped him a hundred-dollar bill with a promise of another he pocketed it and agreed without hesitation to do what she asked.

Only two sheikhs and no woman resided in the suites, he informed her. He also agreed to leave the cabin door ajar if and when both sheikhs took an afternoon nap and to buzz her in her cabin when the coast was clear for her to come up and take a peek.

Her motive was of no interest to him whatsoever, his years at sea as a butler had prepared him for any peculiarity of taste shown by cruise passengers.

14

A Pig's Tail

Like any spoilt only piglet Arafat needed routine. Back on the orchard in her native Marseilles her days were regulated. Chef, who to Arafat was both father and mother, would wake her early in the morning, feed her breakfast of two-star Michelin leftovers, hose her down, rub her with a herbal smelling oil and finally put a little collar around her neck before they walked together among the oak trees in the orchard.

Arafat could sniffle and snuffle to her little heart's content. Searching out truffles was to her much like panning for gold. The truffle when she found it was a prize but one she could not eat. Her reward was forthcoming, the more truffles that piled up in chef's basket the better the snacks she received as reward. At the end of the day her greatest pleasure was a happy chef. She would snuggle in his armpit and literally smell his happiness because to Arafat being a truffle pig was her reason for living. And to keep a chef happy is what every little truffle piglet yearns for.

This sudden change of lifestyle called for much adjustment from little Arafat pig. Being carried in a basket from land to sea was a trauma and even though her chef was still around so were many other multi-coloured people. Where once she had been the centre of his universe, now it seemed she was an afterthought. And in the corners of her little piggy mind seeds of self-doubt took root.

In this strange place, full of noise and people, there were no oak trees at all to speak of. Other than walking her on a leash around a wooden deck with unfamiliar swooshing noises all round chef paid her scant attention and she spent her time, as it seemed to her, inside and underground. She still slept beside chef in her basket but for the most part she was handled by the boy, the boy who smelt of cumin and other exotic spices and spent time on his knees mumbling, the boy who fed her but who seemed to like her one minute and to dislike her the next.

Habits once established in a pig as in a person are very hard to break. And affection once experienced is hard to do without. Arafat the truffle pig, the chef's all time favorite, could live without much sunlight and endure the bustle of the galley but she could not do without a pat from the chef for a truffle. She could not do without her truffle hunt.

A truffle pig's snout is an awesome instrument. On board a cruise ship smells are for the most part trapped within its hull and to a truffle pig this becomes a smorgasbord. During the afternoons, when the chef dozed and Mahmoud prayed, Arafat would go into the corridor and sniff. It was during this siesta time that Arafat got a whiff of a familiar odour. Not quite the musky, earthy fungal odour of truffle she knew well, but similar. The door to chef's cabin was always left ajar and Arafat was usually leashed but today the leash hung loose. Eager to bring chef a truffle, Arafat followed her snout out of the cabin and snuffled her way along the corridor to the lift. On a sea day, the ship snoozed, passengers digested while crew prepared for the evening rush so few were around to see a small pink pig trailing a leash trot inside the crew's lift and hide in a corner.

A cabin steward, too busy picking his nose to look down, did the honors and pushed the button. The lift transported the steward and Arafat to the upper deck. Both emerged from the lift unaware of the other. The steward headed fore and Arafat took two more noisy snuffles and headed aft.

Arafat snuffled her way along a carpeted corridor until she caught a blast of that odour wafting on the air conditioning into the passageway from under the door of Sheikh Hasim's suite. She pushed it with her snout, pushed harder and the door opened easily. The door had been left un-snibbed by Sanchez Mendez, the cabin's butler, for Major Barbara who had paid him a hundred dollars to leave the door unlocked and another hundred if she gained access.

Sheikh Hasim lay snoring gently, blowing bubbles through puce lips, spreadeagled on his bed in his underpants and socks, his naked hairy chest, like a carpet of moss, rose and fell as though in a gentle breeze. To a pig in a foreign environment the sheikh's hairy chest resembled the forest floor around the oak trees. She followed her small pink snout to a foot in a sock that projected over the side of the bed and sniffed. There was the faintest touch of 'that smell' about the sock but not enough to promise a successful truffle hunt.

She raised her small pink head and sniffed at an open doorway then followed her snout. Lying naked but for black woollen socks was the sheikh's double, the actor Sebastian. Sebastian may have been known for his good looks before he exchanged them for the sheikh's but none of his serial girlfriends would have or could have endorsed his personal hygiene.

The pig felt a surge of recognition; she was back in her comfort zone. There on the carpet in all their glory was a pair of underpants across the seat of which was written 'superhero.' Arafat approached with caution but caution changed to eagerness because the truffle smell was there. She raised her head and sniffed again. This time she honed in on Sebastian's black woollen socks, socks that gave out an even stronger luscious aroma. She grasped the corner of the sock in her mouth and pulled. Two more tugs and off came the sock. Deeply asleep and lost in dreams of an old amour, Sebastian smiled and wriggled his toes. Arafat loaded the sock on top of the underpants and tried them on for bite size. Yes, she could easily carry them both back to chef's cabin.

But greed can often overcome and instead of counting her blessings Arafat went back for seconds. As she tugged at Sebastian's other sock he opened his eyes and yelled.

The scream from his double woke the sheikh. As he scrambled for his robe he saw a small pig disappearing through his cabin door and, in the excitement of the moment, also thought he saw the very plain, short, thickset woman who had greeted them on deck that very morning, disappear quickly out of sight.

She was not a woman of a physical appearance that Sheikh Hasim usually remembered; she presented no potential for a little Western dalliance. But why, he wondered was she standing at his open cabin door? Why had she earlier approached them once on deck and another time at breakfast? Perhaps she was a sort of female sexual pervert. He brushed the moment off as an optical illusion, a figment of his imagination.

Major Barbara Cock stood at the open cabin door, frozen to the spot by a bloodcurdling scream from inside. She thought she heard the word 'fuck' yelled in an accented English so ducked behind the door before scurrying off along the corridor in the wake of the small pink pig.

The sheikh was willing to swear when later questioned that the pig was fully grown and weighed around a hundred kilo. He also attested that the pig was carrying something black in its huge and apparently blood-soaked jaws. He ordered a second lock be put on his cabin door.

Chef Armand, a heavy afternoon sleeper, dreamt on through Arafat's arrival back in his cabin, her leash still trailing and her prize of truffle underpants and sock in her mouth. She carefully deposited her prize at the foot of his bed and exposed her tummy to him, ready for a pat.

15

————

Man to Man

Arafat grew in stature as news of her passed from mouth to mouth starting with Sheikh Hasim. By the time details of what had happened reached the ear of the captain the piglet had morphed into a boar of around a hundred kilos with giant tusks and had attacked the sheikh while he slept.

Captain Svensen had three loves, vodka, sardines and a quiet life, so naturally he avoided any form of trouble. He and the chef had travelled many nautical miles together so it seemed to the good Swedish captain that they should discuss this man to man. He prepared two vodka glasses and opened some sardines, fixed his face to neutral and waited. He knew from the start there would be trouble because the knock on his cabin door was not a tap it was a thump. Chef, like many of his profession, could verge on hysteria. The captain took shelter behind his desk and bleated, 'Come.'

The chef did not come alone. With him was a small pink pig, which he led on a leash. In his other hand he held a pair of underpants and a sock, which he deposited on the desk in front of Captain Svensen. By the set of chef's chin and the clench of his teeth it was apparent he was ruffled. A purple hue around his cheeks reminded the captain of the rim of an active volcano. He decided silence was the best policy.

The captain poured two hefty vodkas and handed one to chef along with a sardine on a biscuit.

The chef gulped down his drink and fed the biscuit and sardine to Arafat.

'She is small for a hundred kilo pig,' the captain observed politely.

Chef hiccupped with anxiety and stroked unseen creases from his white trousers. 'My country is being taken over,' he announced. 'I have no say over the dreadful wailing I have to listen to several times a day which, to make matters worse, comes over a loudspeaker. My prize truffle pig is under threat. My *haute cuisine* is under threat. I have no rights here, I have no rights in France.'

He paused for breath and the captain refilled his glass.

'Take me with my pig or not at all.'

He stopped for another breath and to down his vodka. The captain nodded sympathetically. Have I overstepped the mark, the chef wondered, worried for an instant about his pension fund, but the captain's expression had not changed, it remained benign and sympathetic.

'We French,' Chef Armand continued, 'discovered *haute cuisine*, it is our cultural heritage. The first cookbook was written in the sixteenth century and the chef who wrote it used pig fat in his recipes. Imagine that! Pig fat. And these barbarians call my animal filthy. King Louis XIV burst his gasket to show the world that we French are leaders in style and good taste. He hosted banquets in Versailles when the English were still gnawing on bones. He ate off gold plates when the Arabs were eating the balls of a camel.'

'I believe sheep balls are still a delicacy in the Middle East,' the captain could not help but add and then wished he hadn't.

'Take your pick, captain, it is me with my pig or you can find another *chef de cuisine*. And in future I shall keep my menus to *haute cuisine*, not *nouvelle*.' The chef exploded and clenched his fist. 'If they want to get thin, they should go to a health farm.'

As no apology seemed to be forthcoming from the chef for any of his pig's actions, the captain absorbed his vodka and watched the chef change to a healthier shade of pink. It was obvious to the captain that the chef was irreplaceable and the sheikh was not. He suspected the sheikh and the chef shared a flair for the theatrical, but the sheikh and his party were only on board for a week. If chef decided to jump ship then the galley was in trouble for months.

He bit into a sardine biscuit. Should anything come of this he would make up a story for head office. The sheikh would need some compensation; perhaps a day in the spa and free access to the Internet would do the trick, topped up with a bottle of Brut.

'Can you restrict your pig to the galley for the remainder of your term?'

Chef had calmed down and was wondering if he had overdone it. He nodded.

On rare occasions Captain Svensen had an inspirational thought. Such thoughts were few and far between and usually came after watching a Bergman movie for Captain Svensen had suffered at an early age and understood the inner yearnings of the human heart. Hadn't chef mentioned Versailles?

'Perhaps,' the captain lowered his vodka glass and looked chef in the eye, 'perhaps we can do a re-enactment of a genuine Versailles banquet in the ship's dining room if you can manage to plan an authentic menu for a very *haute* night?'

Chef felt a great swelling in his chest as though his heart was fit to burst and put it down to gratitude. For an instant, he would willingly have kissed the captain's feet.

'Of course,' he responded and without another word had disappeared along with his little pink pig.

A good man to man will always do the trick, the captain reflected and wondered how he could make his two guest speakers, Dr Rbib Dji of Mumbai, author of *Find Your Path to Happiness Through Food* and new age cardiologist Simon Schmitz PhD of Big Sur, California, USA, author of *Eat Raw, Live Longer* and *Go Paleo – Cavemen have better sex,* disappear.

* * *

Blame for Arafat's escape into the nether regions of the ship bounced from one head to another, missed Mahmoud entirely and landed squarely on the shoulders of Moroccan sous chef Ahmed, who had objected to the pig from the start. With little bluster Ahmed was dispatched to a lowlier task but not before the disgruntled man had hissed at Mahmoud to 'remember your promise to your uncle.'

Kept in the refrigerator for use upon the buffet tables was the smoked head of a large boar. The head had been the subject of many a joke amongst the kitchen staff. It had suffered many humiliations, been dressed up as a former head of state, had worn a captain's uniform, headdresses of many types and nationalities and even at one stage had doubled as Marilyn Monroe in a blonde wig. Even with no dressing up to speak of at a distance it resembled Edward G Robinson. Empowered by his man-to-man with Captain Svensen, the chef ordered the butcher to retrieve the boar's head from the freezer.

'Put sunglasses on him,' he bellowed to his astonished kitchen staff and tied the black and white scarf around the pig's head. The thought of the two sheikhs who occupied the captain's table nightly staring at the buffet pig made chef first smile then roar with laughter.

16

Jerome

For the second time in forty-eight hours Captain Svensen was faced with problems. This time the main dining area was the source of the problem.

The captain took pride in his dining-room staff and in particular Jerome, the *maître d'* whom he would describe as faultless. Schooled by the company to pave the way for smooth sailing for passengers with a list of needs as long as the Bayeux Tapestry he never forgot a passenger's name and was immediately attuned to their dining habits as far as tables were concerned. He handled his waiting staff like kindergarten children, tending to their concerns like a Mother Hubbard. His face was rock solidly fixed in a look so sublime that even the Mona Lisa would feel challenged by it. So for Jerome to stand before the captain pulling plaintively at his white gloves and wearing a scowl, things must be at an all-time low in the dining room,

Captain Svensen came around his desk and stood with Jerome as a sign of solidarity. Jerome was teetotal so offering him vodka at ten in the morning would not have helped the issue.

'The situation is becoming difficult,' Jerome explained in a nasal voice conditioned through having to speak through a smile. 'This being a wellness cruise they all want special orders but the chef won't budge. They want low fat, or lactose free, or this or that and chef won't do it and so my staff are suffering.'

The captain thought for a moment and guiltily suggested, 'Let them fib a little? Who is to know if the sauces contain butter or margarine or if the cream is reduced or full fat? Aren't we always told that the passenger knows best?'

'But…' Jerome squinted artfully as though the idea was not too bad, 'how can I tell the staff to fib to everyone?'

A tap on the door announced the arrival of the newly appointed *sous chef*, the Scotsman Hamish, a union man through and through who also had his axe to grind.

'Chef's suffering some sort of breakdown,' he suggested, 'and we in the kitchen think he needs some professional help. Not that keeping a pet pig in the galley bothers any of us, though my old granny would turn in her kirk, but it seems the chef is on the way to going *bonkerrrrs*. After all, 'he continued, 'you cannot dress up the buffet boar's head in one of those white scarf things that the Arabs wear and sunglasses and put it on the table as a centrepiece, now can ye? And when the Indian gentleman who's lecturing on board made a few suggestions chef threatened him with a crepe pan, not to mention the American gent with the whiskers and the ponytail who tried to convince chef to serve potatoes raw. I thought chef would burst a gasket.'

The captain was well aware that Chef Armand was travelling along a razor's edge but at their man-to-man the chef seemed comfortable with the idea of a Versailles dinner and he only needed to keep chef happy for another thirty days after which he could hopefully replace him if by then he hadn't sent the shipping company broke. He would deal with the guest lecturers but a further insult thrown at the sheikh could possibly break the camel's back.

It was Jerome who came up with what could be an answer.

'If chef's got issues, then that lady passenger, Major Cock, isn't she a psychiatrist? Maybe she could chat with chef and sort him out?'

And so it was that within the hour Barbara received a message asking would she be so kind as to attend the captain in his cabin at a time that suited her best about a matter of some urgency.

17

A Major Decision

Meeting up with Captain Svensen was something Barbara could well do without. Her mind was fixed on finding the identity of Sheikh Hasim's double. But, as can be expected after years of army training, a summons from a man of rank could not be ignored. What she was to discover from this untimely meeting was that help can often come from most unexpected quarters.

The captain looking resplendent in his whites opened the door in response to her knock and ushered her inside and she instinctively saluted. This unexpected token of respect came as a surprise to the humbled captain who was more used to sniggers from his crew. He pulled out a chair for the major woman and proceeded to cut to the chase. The major may have noticed, he pointed out, that the menu on board ship was not as extensive as one would expect.

It was not the menu that Barbara was aware of. She held her breath; she could anticipate what was coming next.

'Is it the chef?' She pre-empted him. 'I sort of got a feeling from the shape of his gravy that he may be having a crisis.'

On the first night, when captain had graciously invited her on to his table, the shape of the gravy puddle around the lamb chops served to her by chef had given her an insight into a troubled mind, she explained.

Captain Svensen was not one to be blinded by authority, nor one to assume that a psychiatrist is necessarily saner than most and this diagnosis based on a puddle of gravy he thought bordered on insanity. Best, he decided, to fill in the dots. The reason he had called her in was because of an incident that had occurred the previous afternoon. A pig had infiltrated the cabin of a sheikh; a regular passenger who this time around it appears was travelling with a double. The pig escaped with a pair of underpants and a sock belonging either to the sheikh or to his double. That was of no consequence because neither man had asked for the clothing to be returned. The good captain paused to open a drawer in his desk and from it withdrew the items of clothing in question, which he handed to Major Barbara Cock.

Major Barbara glanced at the clothing and felt a tremor of excitement, not because of the clothing but the implication.

The captain continued to explain. Chef Armand, their executive chef owned the pig and it appeared he feared for the animal's life because of a conflict of interests with a local imam. For this reason, the chef had brought his pig on board and somehow it escaped and entered the sheikh's suite.

The captain took a breather and a swig of vodka as he bent down to close the desk drawer. This problem, which Chef Armand left behind on shore, seemed to have haunted him in such a way that his behaviour on board was troubling the galley and the dining-room staff, the captain explained.

'What happened when the pig broke into the sheikh's cabin?' Barbara Cock enquired.

'Well,' the captain explained, his face a mask of modesty, 'the sheikh was most understanding and has forgotten the incident. He and his double will enjoy a day in the spa with our compliments.'

This was the best news Barbara had heard since learning that the sheikh had a double. It meant they would both be enjoying the joys of the spa with only bathrobes separating Barbara from the give-away tattoo on the left buttock cheek of the double. Opportunities to peek and observe their bare behinds were sure to present themselves during massages, facials, sauna, exfoliations and spells in the spa pool if only she could get access. Barbara managed to curb her enthusiasm and steady her voice as she asked, 'So what would you like me to do about the chef?'

The captain stuttered with embarrassment as he asked this gracious if unattractive woman to spend some of her vacation counselling his troubled chef.

'Would you be so kind as – of course there would be remuneration – could you, as soon as possible, but don't let him know –'

Major Barbara Cock nodded agreement and stemmed the captain's flow with one quick question, 'Have the sheikh and his double taken up your kind offer of a day in the spa?'

The captain thought this was an unusual segue', but then this was a woman who read things into the shape of gravy. And, after all, she did salute him.

'Yes, I booked them in myself for the next sea day.'

Eager to shift the worry of a troubling chef from his own shoulders on to the major's he thanked her and as an afterthought and as a way of showing his gratitude asked if she would also like to spend a day in the spa.

Anyone who has known the luxury of a cruise will know that a day in the spa is the icing on the cake. Anyone that is but Major Barbara Cock, who was raised by her military father and her servicemen brothers to believe that a good scrub down with soap and a long run is what it takes to make the skin glow. A further spell as an army psychiatrist more than confirmed it. So it was with caution that she approached the spa later that day to make a booking that would coincide with that of the sheikh and his double. This was definitely enemy territory: this was not her comfort zone.

She emerged from the lift and followed her nose to double glass doors, to the whiff of fragrant oils and heady scents. Two snooty beauticians in pink cracked a smile in her direction. This would not be easy. She presented her gift voucher for a day of spa goodies to the less self-involved of the two beauticians, the one who actually stopped doing her nails. On seeing the captain's signature the beautician's smile broadened slightly.

'Two of my friends are booked in for the day, Sheikh Hasim and his friend?'

A faint wrinkle marred the beautician's perfect facescape as she thumbed through a huge appointment book.

'Yes, Sheikh Hasim for two, the couple's package. The day after tomorrow, they are having the mud wrap, hot stone massage, Thai massage and sauna. We can't have you on the same program as we only have two operators on the body work, but we can work on your face.' She attempted to raise a Botoxed eyebrow.

'What about the sauna?' Major Barbara queried.

'Are you non-binary, because the sauna is not mixed?'

She openly stared at Major Barbara's khaki shorts and shirt and severe hairstyle.

Barbara thought she had heard every known term to describe a person's gender but non-binary was a new one. Under the circumstances, she decided to opt for no definite gender orientation and nodded, then added 'gender queer' to avoid any misunderstanding.

The beautician raised her pen to make an entry and again the fateful Botoxed eyebrow struggled to ask a silent question.

'Cock,' Major Barbara advised. 'Major Barbara Cock, cabin 456.'

It was done and dusted. Major Barbara Cock and the two sheikh would enjoy a day at the spa together, or so Barbara hoped.

18

Analyze This

Chef now felt that life had a purpose. He had an important dinner to prepare for. Not just any dinner but a Versailles dinner that would represent everything stylish that was French, or as French as France used to be.

Very few of his galley staff were French trained and fewer still spoke the language. His new *sous chef* was a Scot from Fife and apart from the *plongeur* Mahmoud and the deposed *sous chef* Ahmed the rest were mainly Asian. Only Ahmed and Mahmoud read a reasonable French and chef needed to research old French recipes. The next day being a shore day was an opportunity to put both to work on the computers. 'You will spend tomorrow searching the net for seventeenth century French recipes,' Armand instructed the pair as they washed down the cutting tables.

Chef had never married, had not even been close. Life at sea presented difficulties to any relationship; few women liked to live alone for months on end. As chef thumbed through his recipes he allowed his mind to wander. Perhaps things would be different with a change of lifestyle, but then what woman wanted a man in his forties that slept with a truffle pig? His one regret was not having a son. Other than his nephew, his sister's child, now living in Japan, his nearest and dearest was a truffle pig.

If there were a common place of prayer on the board the ship it would likely find the crew on their knees praying that most of the passengers leave the ship tomorrow on the first shore day. This could be said in particular of the galley staff that only now had been told about the Versailles dinner. They had five days to plan and implement this feast, which would take place on the final night of the voyage. The upside was that the French speakers were to do the research while the rest of the galley staff were free to prowl the Riviera. Only chef, Ahmed and Mahmoud would remain to slap some food on the table for any passengers who stayed on board,

Mahmoud had never felt a sense of belonging in his uncle's household where his cousins inevitably came first and his aunt was merely a black shadow that did nothing but cook. His mother had long since run off with a Frenchman and brought shame to his father's name. As a result, his father, who had no job to speak of, had gone back to Tunisia so the only home that Mahmoud ever knew was the shack beside the mosque in the village near chef's orchard.

Now, for the first time in his life, Mahmoud felt special. It was his responsibility to mind chef's truffle pig and because he could read and write in French he had the special task of helping with this dinner. He felt chosen, but was he chosen by chef to be better than the others in the galley or was he chosen by his uncle to rid the world of a truffle pig? To do or not to do, that was the question. As he wiped down the cutting bench he reflected on the turn of events that had made him face such a moral dilemma.

Meanwhile, chef was soon to face his own demons. He was about to take a break when a short, broad woman in khaki came into the galley and headed his way. Chef was unused to passengers entering his domain and this woman marched, head held high, as though on a parade ground. He hoped she was not yet another food expert.

'Barbara Cock,' the woman introduced herself and extended a blunt fingered hand. 'And you sir must be the executive chef Armand?'

Chef preened at her use of his title.

'The captain suggested we talk about the Versailles dinner you are planning, I'm to write a piece for my paper, I am a travel and food writer you see.'

A food writer! Chef felt as though his ship had at last come home. He beamed and took her blunt fingers in his, his head bowed in mock humility.

'Some time tomorrow as I am planning on remaining on board?'

Barbara decided the chef would be an easy egg to crack

'As am I,' was chef's response and, in the time it takes to fry that egg, a meeting was agreed upon for after the breakfast rush was over. The chef's spell upon a psychiatrist's couch was about to begin.

* * *

Demoted *sous chef* Ahmed, who was about to research recipes with Mahmoud, also had dilemmas to solve. He prayed at the same mosque led by Mahmoud's uncle the imam, a regular busybody who had long been aware that Ahmed worked on the same cruise ship as his enemy Chef Armand and could be asked to keep an eye on his nephew Mahmoud. But what Ahmed had observed to date of Mahmoud's attitude to the truffle pig was causing him great concern; Mahmoud had grown too fond of the little pig.

19

To The Galley Bound

Early the next morning the *Pacific Belle* tied up in St Tropez. The albatross flapped its wings and cawed and watched from his perch above the upper deck as the ship settled in to a berth as a horse would into a stall after a long race. Waiting as it were to be hosed down and cleaned up.

In St Tropez, as with all the ports along this stretch of coast, the sun always shone, the gardens were greener, the flowers bloomed, the shops sold more luxuries, the sands on the beaches were whiter, the bathing suits briefer and the women more beautiful. The passenger stairs were driven into place and one by one or two by two the passengers disembarked for their fix of glamour or simply to feel solid earth beneath their feet. From their vantage points on the lower decks, crew not designated to turn the hose on their tired ship waited eagerly for the stream of passengers to end because then it would be their turn to disembark.

The galley staff had cleaned up after breakfast and the galley shone and echoed in its emptiness. At the far end of the galley chef had set up his computer and positioned Ahmed and Mahmoud in front of it.

Ahmed turned a harsh black eye towards Mahmoud, brushed breadcrumbs from his beard, clicked on Google and hissed at Mahmoud, 'Type in *truffle pigs – getting rid of.*'

Mahmoud, well used to following orders, did as he was told. *Killing for truffles*, was the screen's response.

Ahmed elbowed Mahmoud aside and typed in, *Poisons that leave no trace.*

When Major Barbara Cock arrived she saw a man and the boy intent on something on a computer screen but the chef was nowhere to be seen. The two were well into the research but something about their demeanor troubled her. The older man repeatedly leaned towards the younger and thumped him on the head. The boy sat hunched up and reluctant as he typed on the keyboard. The older was swarthy and bearded and the younger dark and fresh-faced. Peering over their shoulder she saw the page heading *How to build a bomb from common kitchen materials.*

Suddenly, sensing her presence, the older of the pair immediately cleared the screen and typed in, *Pâté on a base of lard or pig fat.* At that moment the chef bounded into the galley. He saw Barbara and waved.

'Coffee?' He indicated the couple at the computer, 'my staff are researching recipes for the very dinner you are writing about – recipes from seventeenth-century France.'

Major Barbara was by nature no alarmist but researching making of bombs in a ship's galley did not bode well. No point in sending chef over the edge, she reasoned; they may have been researching a bomb at his request. After all, the shape of the gravy he spooned on her chops was troubling.

They moved up to a ship's café and settled in. The interview went well until Barbara asked the chef about his future. That somehow touched a nerve and, like an egg cracked on the side of a pan, chef revealed the very yoke of his existence and his whole sordid story tumbled out into the waiting ears of a psychiatrist.

The story about the nasty imam who threatened to kill his pig, the story of chef's bad case of tinnitus and how the mosque's loudspeakers made it worse, the case for noise pollution. Of the passengers with their ridiculous dietary needs, of the sheikh who insults pork, of all the experts who claim to know what is healthy to eat and what is not. As much as Major Barbara thought him barking mad, she could see the logic in his argument.

Major Barbara's moral compass clicked into gear. Listening to chef describe the sound of the crackling loudspeaker, she mentally and emotionally slid into his shoes. She understood quiet time as a human need. Every afternoon she lay down on the floor (to give her spine support) and lifted her legs to ninety degrees, and thus she would stay for at least an hour to allow a shifting of her blood supply. As she imagined herself in this position she allowed herself to drift into a nether land until into her quiet time came the wailing sound chef had described that went on and on through a crackling loudspeaker until eventually it faded to a bleeping stop.

Realising his dilemma, she felt a pang of empathy for his situation. *He is an artist and a kind man who loves pigs, loves his art of cooking*, she told herself. *Like me, he is a patriot who loves his country*. She felt sorry for the chef and knew in her heart of hearts that she would help him in any way she could. In the meantime, he really needed to get his act together and carry out the role of executive chef at least until the end of the month. Perhaps a few happy pills would help. As for his kitchen staff and the two researchers looking at bomb making on the chef's computer, that was another matter entirely.

Chef let out a long sigh. His talk with this charming food writer seemed to relieve his tensions. One should always look beneath a person's surface, he decided. *This woman has no chic, no style, she is not thin and has the shoulders of a weightlifter,* and he mused. *As for her hair, Mon dieu! But she has a soul and I think she understands. I shall cook for her whatever she requests, even nouvelle cuisine.*

She interrupted his reverie. 'I would love to put that angle into my story. How would Louis himself have planned a Versailles dinner with his chef?'

'*Mon dieu*, I love it,' he gushed.

With his faith in human nature partly restored, chef agreed to try some of her soothing pills, one at night with water, and to provide her with the menu for the Versailles dinner as soon as it was decided upon for her travel article. Air kissing, they parted company with his hope expressed that they might meet again soon.

20

No Sure Fix

Goldfarb had no need for a shore fix. As much as he loved St Tropez he was happy to prowl the ship for gambling buddies. The casino was quiet and in the light of day looked tired. The croupier and a waiter were deep into a game of scrabble. Goldfarb ordered a coffee and grabbed a magazine, settling in for a day of peace and quiet. The dim light in the deserted casino suited his demeanor; he hated sunlight and wore dark glasses around the clock.

The tranquility of the moment was broken by the sound of squeaking, which turned out to be a Zimmer frame with Maurice the bridge player in the driver's seat. The Zimmer frame and Maurice proceeded slowly across the expanse of soiled carpet headed straight for the blackjack table. Over the squeak a voice an octave higher questioned, 'anything happening here?'

The croupier turned his attention to the elderly man. 'No bridge today, it's a shore day. You want to play blackjack?' and before Goldfarb's dunked biscuit could crumble, a second figure, in jeans and cashmere with a ponytail of shoulder length grey hair, swaggered into the casino.

Goldfarb recognised Dirk von Klimt, the lecturer in fine art, as the newcomer sashayed up to the blackjack table and purred a 'Deal me in' in the mellow voice of George Sanders.

The shrunken Maurice looked up from his Zimmer frame through thick glasses and nodded but made no move to stake the table. Goldfarb brushed away the biscuit crumbs and stood to join the action. Dirk bet heavily and played hard, and Goldfarb read an adrenalin rush in the flush on his cheeks. The very best type to make a killing from – the gambling addict.

Goldfarb moved in to join the table but was battered aside by a Zimmer frame moving with the speed of a racing car. He tried to make eye contact with Maurice to warn him off but the message bounced off the thick lenses like a wrongly addressed email.

Goldfarb took a back seat and watched. Dirk eyed off his opponent and smothered a grin but then the surprises began. Like a night owl scanning a forest floor for mice Maurice did not take his eyes off the cards and hedged his bets as though he knew what was coming.

Goldfarb got the picture. *The old guy counts the cards. He knows what's been played and what's left to play.*

The croupier was looking worried but Dirk played on regardless as chip after chip was slid across to Maurice. The pile in front of Maurice threatened to collapse and bury him but Dirk had the bug and wanted to win his losses back.

'Fool.' thought Goldfarb. 'Bloody fool,' his mother echoed in his ear.

The game eventually came to a halt when the thin voice of Maurice announced from behind the stack of chips, 'Waterworks are calling, gents, I'd better be off,' and the Zimmer frame and Maurice and the pile of chips miraculously disappeared, headed for the gentleman's toilet.

* * *

'He knows to get out when he's winning,' the voice of Goldfarb's mother chanted in his ear.

Dirk had turned a nasty shade of purple and changed more big notes for chips. Goldfarb swore he could hear the adrenalin pumping through Dirk's veins as he moved in for the kill.

The bloodbath lasted for more than an hour by which time Goldfarb was considerably richer and

Dirk von Klimt, the auctioneer of fine and fake art, was considerably poorer. While Maurice the bridge player with the Zimmer frame carried less fluids and substantially more cash.

It turned out that Dirk was no favourite of the croupier since a previous voyage when he sold him a fake painting as a genuine article that the croupier later saw on sale on the pavement beside Hyde Park. From behind his hand the croupier whispered to Goldfarb, 'It's the game of bridge. They train to know what cards are played, don't say I didn't warn you.'

Dirk limped back to his cabin like an injured athlete beaten by an old man on a Zimmer frame and a yid from New York in gold chains and dark glasses. He knew gambling was his weakness but when that hunger overcame him he was left with no choice but to feed it; the adrenalin fixes came only from winning.

He would show them. Tomorrow at the auction he would show them. He would blind them with rhetoric, smother them with art speak they could never understand, he would work on their greed, massage their need to make a profit; he would sell them a gamble but this time he would win. He shook out his mane of grey hair and pawed the carpet with his Nike like a stallion ready to mount. He would make back every cent he had lost. He would hone his skills at rhetoric and part these greedy passengers from their money.

From his closet he withdrew a small painting of a white tree. In his heart of hearts he knew that this small landscape, this Japanese tree, would do the trick.

21

St. Tropez

While Dirk von Klimt mourned his losses and Goldfarb counted his winnings Sheikh Hasim and his double meandered along the foreshore of St Tropez, the sheikh loudly protesting about the decadent western women in G-string bikinis that littered the beach like a Barbie doll convention.

'Our women are modest,' he proclaimed and stopped to watch as a blonde in a G-string stood up.

'Do they have a choice?' Sebastian wondered. He came from a litter of three strong-minded sisters.

Sheikh Hasim waved a ringed hand over the smorgasbord of firm brown legs and rounded bottoms and cascades of hair. 'These women have no modesty; they leave nothing to be imagined. This is what happens when you let a woman have a driver's licence, she will strip naked on a beach and find lovers. We do not allow a woman to drive her own car unescorted, we do not let them invite temptation.'

Sebastian smothered a smile when he thought of his sisters and their husbands. The girls ruled their men with iron fists.

Dogs were as numerous as people on the St Tropez foreshore. So busy was the sheikh gazing at the woman in the G-string that he stepped in the recently deposited droppings of a standard poodle. As he attempted to scrape his shoe free of debris Sebastian reflected on their conversation. If every woman Sebastian knew had been blanketed from head to toe in black then perhaps he too would find the current scene inviting. Sebastian, the youngest in a family of three sisters and the only boy was well conditioned to seeing the female form in different stages of undress so he took the scene for granted and simply appreciated the beauty laid out before him.

The sheikh on the other hand found this much like walking past the chocolate counter at Harrods. Sebastian could swear the sheikh was drooling.

Just when the smell of tanning oil was becoming suffocating, a bigger broader, older, version of a Barbie doll came heading their way. Sebastian recognised her instantly. It was Pamela Lawson-Groves III, the woman from the casino, the one with the legs and a fast food chain of restaurants. For a moment Sebastian was tempted to hide and then he remembered his words of caution to the woman not to blow his cover in public. So he held his breath and prayed.

'Do we not know this irritating woman from the ship? Is it not her company that intends to sell us southern fried chicken?' Sheikh Hasim enquired. 'Do you not find it amusing that she thinks our Pakistani workforce will eat fried chicken instead of a curry or a good Shawarma kebab with humus? These Americans!' He giggled and repeated, 'These Americans' in a loud voice as she passed.

To his surprise, this dominating western woman, one who held no more appeal to him than a hump-backed whale, passed him by without a sideways glance refusing to take his bait or provide him with a juicy confrontation. She just kept walking as though he were invisible. The sheikh blinked in amazement. She must have heard him unless she wore a hearing aid. Like any male with a substantial ego he found this snub made her all the more desirable. As he watched her disappear he noted that her legs were long and shapely. Sebastian heaved a sigh of relief. He felt like whooping with joy. He would contact the woman later, this must not happen again.

When Pamela, like Lot's wife, dared to look back, she observed one sheikh was seated and the other knelt to wipe something off the other's shoe. She wondered, would a sheikh wipe something off a double's shoe? She was put in mind of the Pope, a firm favourite of hers, who regularly washed the feet of the poor and humble. The sheikh she met in the casino was a humble man, Pamela concluded, it could be him on his knees. She thought it would be hard to tell them apart and hoped she would hear from the real sheikh soon. She rather fancied him. Would he live in a mansion in the desert, she wondered, or a penthouse in a glass building in Dubai, with a view of the Arabian Sea?

* * *

For Sheikh Hasim there were two necessities of life, a hookah and his time alone. And all he wanted after time in St Tropez was exactly that. Growing up as one of a multiple of siblings he learned very early the precious value of privacy. Unfortunately, on this voyage he had neither. His doctor had suggested he cut down on the hookah and his double put a kybosh on his being alone.

So it was no surprise that by the third day at sea Sheikh Hasim was treading on thin ice. One pack of Camels that he had so far managed to resist sat unopened by his bedside. He blamed the morning in St Tropez, and the explosion of semi-naked western women for his feeling of restlessness, aided and abetted as they were by his double, a rather stupid impoverished actor who sat watching TV soaps all day. Sebastian was slumped before the TV screen his head drooped forward.

The idiot could sleep on a camel's hump, Hasim observed. He would hide behind a magazine up on deck and enjoy a cigarette, not quite a hookah of hashish but it would do, and some badly needed time alone. He would speak to no one. It was that or he would go quite mad.

Hasim reached for the Camels and a copy of *Playboy* and headed out on deck alone. The deck was deserted. Most passengers had stayed ashore. Hasim sank down on to a day bed and fumbled eagerly with the packet of Camels. He had wives to open packets, to remove cellophane, otherwise why pay for manicures, but on this occasion he struggled with the cellophane alone. It felt tougher than a camel's saddlebag. Finally he managed to puncture the cellophane with his teeth. He opened the packet and withdrew a cigarette. He ran it below his ample nose and sniffed. Delicious. A lighter? It dawned on him that no one was around to light his cigarette and he never lit his own, this was usually Habibi's task or the double's.

As he sat with his unopened *Playboy*, an unlit Camel cigarette dangling between his puce lips, a long thin hand with crimson nails reached out to him holding a Zippo lighter. Flick! A single spark followed by a flame. Sheikh Hasim puffed hungrily on his ignited Camel and saw through the billow of smoke the smiling face of Pamela Lawson-Groves III.

'I didn't say hello this morning in case I gave the game away,' she stage whispered and landed squarely on the end of the day bed her behind close to Sheikh Hasim's sandaled feet.

The Sheikh took most things literally.

'What game? He asked politely.

'You know,' the woman winked with one eye.

The wink, a Western mode of communication, was entirely lost on Sheikh Hasim. *Did she have something in her eye or was she saying something?* He mused.

Perhaps she has a twitch, but good legs nevertheless, he silently observed.

She lifted the *Playboy* from his chest and opened it. 'My, you are a naughty sheikh.' She had begun to blink with one eye often and smiled a lot. 'No wonder you've never married.'

The woman has fast food restaurants but nothing between the ears this must be caused by a bad diet or dead husbands, the sheikh concluded.

He hastened to correct her. 'Of course I am married, madam, I have four wives.'

Pamela had brought down more defences than Sir Winston Churchill. A man who pretends to be married to take himself off the marriage market was a ploy she knew well. *Lighten up* She told herself, *he's running scared.*

'Then a lot has happened since the other night,' joked Pamela. 'Now tell me about your houses and I'll tell you about mine.' This angle had worked with him last time.

'I have five houses, one for each wife, and one for myself and they are close together to make things easier for me,' Sheikh Hasim advised in a monotone. 'I have four houses and a penthouse.' He wondered why he was being so specific but letting it all hang out, as he had seen on Oprah, that opinionated host of the talk show on American TV was the way of the western world.

She didn't wait to be asked. 'Well I have three houses and they are far apart, Salt Lake City, Dallas and Washington DC. And I live in all three – but I've always wanted to live in the desert.'

'Then I hope one day you do,' he responded rather tartly as he puffed angrily on the cigarette and billowed smoke. Now that she was obviously coming on to him he found her unattractive and annoying. Eager to finish his cigarette and be alone he slid his feet out from under Pamela Lawson-Groves, picked up his *Playboy* magazine, nodded at the woman and walked away.

He thought he heard her yell out after him, 'But we both run restaurants, we have so much to talk about.'

He spent the next hour hidden away in a corner on A-deck chain smoking Camels, observed closely by the ship's albatross from a perch above him but protected from its droppings by a canvas canopy.

When later he returned to his suite he found Sebastian in a state of agitation. He assured his double that his quick fix on deck had done no harm. The only person that had come across him was that noisy blonde

American from the morning trip to St Tropez, but he soon got rid of her.

By now Sebastian had moved mentally into one of Pamela's houses and handed in his notice to the troublesome sheikh, so he did what doubles do when they are caught off guard, he did a double take. Whatever damage had been done to his intended romance with a cougar he must undo and undo as soon as was possible.

When Pamela returned to her cabin she found a message was waiting for her from the sheikh inviting her to meet him in the Jazz Bar the following night at midnight and not to call but just turn up.

She was puzzled. On deck he seemed entirely different from the night they met in the casino but obviously he was having trouble keeping his emotions in check. A man of wealth couldn't be too careful, she figured. Women would want him for his money, whereas she, well, she had money of her own.

Pamela had many occupations in her time but the study of reflexology was the one that stood her in good stead in helping to break down barriers put up by the male species against domestic bliss. No man of whatever race or age could resist a woman who cooked well and showed interest in his feet. No two big toes were ever alike, this much she knew, and this much was proven.

To give a reading of a man's big toe held just as much mystique as the reading from a pack of tarot cards.

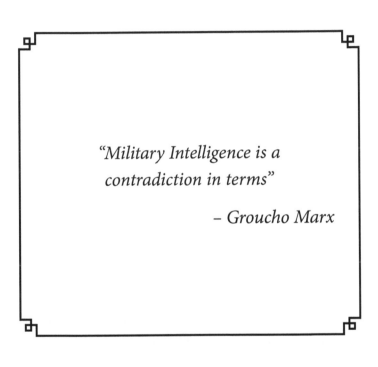

"Military Intelligence is a contradiction in terms"

– Groucho Marx

22

A View Of The Rear

Major Barbara Cock usually worked her assassinations
to a rigid plan. She would work out beforehand what
method she would use and much depended upon the
situation and terrain. Getting her target alone was the
first challenge and this was the challenge she needed
to overcome in identifying the real sheikh and not
the fake. She left her cabin in a bathrobe and headed
for the spa. Initially she had planned to smother the
sheikh. With the intrusion of a double it seemed more
sensible to drug the sheikh then push him overboard
in the dead of night, but lately she was considering
poison. Several different poisons could be administered
without leaving a trace.

A challenging day lay ahead, one in which she
needed to stay alert for opportunities to catch a glimpse

of the sheikh and his double undressed, a task she had to perform cautiously. The less her targets were aware of her the better. Ever since the incident with the pig when she was seen looking through their open door the sheikhs had pointedly avoided her. No point in arousing their suspicions. Time to tread carefully if she wanted the sheikhs to lower their guard as well as their bathrobes.

She arrived at the spa reception in time to see both sheikhs disappear into a massage room followed by two hefty male masseuses dressed in white from top to sandshoes. The bored receptionist from the other day looked through her unknowingly.

'Cock, 456,' Barbara mumbled and the receptionist unflinchingly found her booking. She pressed a buzzer and a tiny Asian beautician led Barbara into a darkened room alight with scented candles.

The beautician replaced Barbara's bathrobe with a wrap and told Barbara to lie down. The beautician slid cushions under certain places, put on some esoteric Eastern music and slapped a thick white sweet-scented goo on Barbara's face and neck. As she started to massage through the thick white goo a voice barked, 'Do the mud thing last' and even the little beautician with her limited English recognised an order when she heard one.

* * *

Despite her resolve to remain alert, Barbara found it very difficult to stay awake. The constant pummeling of her face with different lotions and potions, followed by a semi electric drill with buffer that sounded dangerously like roadworks being done had a startling effect. Barbara was flooded by a warm sensation and as she wafted away she heard in the distance a mild cracking, as though part of a glacier was breaking off and realised that she was hearing her bones relaxing. On and on went the buffing then the massage, all over her face, her neck, her chest, as Barbara sank deeper and deeper into a relaxed state.

There was a sudden twitch and she felt free. Her mind, which usually she held restrained in defined boxes, took off on its own on a backward journey. And as she lay propped up with cushions and covered in white goo, breathing in heavily scented wax and listening to Maharani music, her mind flew back to a certain young recruit named Jenkins.

Jenkins' sergeant major had ordered he undergo a session with Barbara because Jenkins had a problem with following orders. Barbara remembered the boy because he was so puny. The sergeant was on the right track because it became evident to Barbara that Jenkins needed someone to talk to.

Jenkins was an only child of generation X. And the one thing that his parents did well was to disagree. So Jenkins grew up being told to do one thing by his father and another by his mother, usually simultaneously. You would think such an upbringing would create an adult with a mind of his own but Jenkins found that doing nothing was his best course of inaction and the most rewarding way of dealing with most things. To make matters worse, both parents used bribes to get him to do the many things he wouldn't do when he wouldn't do them and used even larger bribes when he continued not to do the things he wouldn't do.

Barbara recognised immediately that little Jenkins was suffering from Pavlov's Dog Syndrome. When she asked him why he had joined the army he answered that he would get lots of orders in the army that he would refuse and as a consequence would be well rewarded for it.

Barbara had treated several other recruits suffering from this same syndrome. Her mind segued back to her own childhood at an order issued by her father, while her mother stood silent. Her mother may well have disagreed but never would she say so, and then if Barbara or her brothers failed to follow orders their father would flick them very hard behind the ear. It hurt and, consequently, everyone followed orders.

As Barbara lay upon the cushioned table she wondered if the flick behind the ear made her follow an order she didn't agree with or whether Jenkins and the other subordinates had benefitted more from being rewarded for doing nothing. There is a divide here she thought as her mind drifted.

What had she recommended as treatment for Jenkins? She remembered telling the sergeant major to flick Jenkins behind the ear when he didn't follow orders and if this didn't work then jab him in the ribs with a rifle butt. *Reconditioning*, she repeated to herself several times until a concerned Asian face leaned in close and asked her if she would like a glass of water.

Sometime in the early afternoon after many layers of creams had finally been absorbed Barbara's little beautician finally said the words *mud facial*. Barbara gathered her scattered wits about her and focused. 'Yes, but do not wash it off, I will do this for myself later.'

So, shortly afterwards when Barbara emerged from the room in her bathrobe and her hair in a turban her face was still covered in mud and she looked very much like Al Jolson at rehearsal. Well disguised, she headed for the relaxation lounge where she would grab a sandwich and if possible a glimpse of the sheikh and his double before and during their sauna.

In the relaxation lounge several people languished in bathrobes around a dip pool and sure enough the sheikh and his double lay side by side on day beds. Barbara kept well away but with a clear view of them both. No one seemed to think a woman with mud on her face to be unusual, after all this was a spa. One sheikh slid off his day lounge and stood. He removed his bathrobe to reveal a pair of patterned underpants, then without much ado walked down the steps into the dip pool. Of course he wouldn't go in naked when women were around. Barbara could see her only opportunity to see the sheikhs without clothes would be in the sauna.

The waiter doing the rounds with exotic drinks seemed to be the signal for the sheikhs to think of the sauna and they departed the dayroom in tandem. Barbara waited a safe period of time and followed them. She pushed open the door of the sauna and peered through the steamy haze. The sheikhs sat alone on the cedar benches, towels draped over their privates. They stirred and were visibly alarmed when Barbara entered and one man held up a hand in protest. Barbara lowered her voice an octave. 'I am non-gender specific' she growled, and draped a towel over her façade.

The sheikh leaned over to Sebastian and asked, 'what the fuck is non-gender specific?' Sebastian, wiser as to the variety of genders in contemporary Western society, responded, 'Not a man and not a woman.'

'Which gender do they prefer?'

'Who knows? Perhaps neither, perhaps both,' Sebastian responded. 'Don't worry about it. I'll protect you.'

Barbara watched them whispering together. *Keep quiet and they may forget about you*, she told herself and settled back in the steam.

Shortly afterwards a bell sounded, an alarm that advised the sheikhs that their time was up.

Barbara was ready. In the pocket of her bathrobe was a pink powder, the type used in India during their Holi Week, when they throw dye on each other to celebrate spring. When she identified the sheikh with the tattoo she would pretend to be Hindu, jump to her feet, throw the pink powder at the double and yell 'Happy Holi.' The dye stayed in the hair for weeks and would cling to a moustache like glue.

She put her hand into the pocket of her bathrobe lying beside her on the bench. She flicked open the container of pink powder and grabbed a handful. She was ready.

The two sheikhs stood. She was right in assuming they would forget about her being there. They let their towels drop and she saw that both were circumcised. They spun around to grab their bathrobes. Barbara gasped: she was faced with two large surgical waterproof sticking plasters, one on the left buttock cheek of both men, entirely obliterating any sign of birthmark or tattoo. How cunning! Barbara, who stood ready for action, sat down. Other than rip off the plaster, which was an obvious no-no, she was no further advanced in identifying who was who than she was before.

One sheikh turned to her and nodded and the other waved and they left the sauna without another backward glance, their bare behinds disrespectfully disappearing through the door.

23

Help

Barbara Cock was not one to give in easily. She had confronted many situations and allowed her moral compass and a female intuition to lead the way, but this assignment was proving costly and claiming expenses without an outcome would be difficult, particularly from a man on an island married to a dog.

Find me something else to tell them apart. The text flew from Barbara's phone straight to the white house on the island. *I cannot get a clear glimpse of the sheikhs' behinds from behind.*

To keep her moral compass honed she tuned into the video Mr Rufus had provided showing the barbarity of live sheep exports to the Middle East. She was, deep down, a sensitive soul and easily affected and she allowed herself to cringe at the fate of the poor sheep.

As an arch manipulator of governments, her client knew exactly how to spur Barbara on. As she lay back and reflected on what to do next a text dinged back to her, which read *Looking into it, may have the solution.*

She had no idea what the message meant but in the meantime she would spend more time in the galley. Something was going on there that was not completely kosher, something that needed her expert eye to observe.

24

Think Louis XIV

By nature, the chef was somewhat of a pedagogue. To an audience of kitchen staff who would not know Versailles from a dog's *derrière* the subject of the day was Louis XIV. It was obvious to chef that if his staff of mainly foreign nationals were to prepare a Versailles dinner then they would need some background information to give it authenticity. With this in mind, he provided seating for his galley throng, the *pâtissier*, the *entremetier*, the *poissonier*, the *garde manger*, the *glacier*, the *confiseur*, the *saucier*, the *bouchier*, Hamish the *sous chef* and various *chef-tournants*. Mahmoud the *plongeur* sat beside chef with Arafat on his lap. Chef mounted a stool and began his lecture:

'King Louis XIV, better known as the Sun King, thought himself a god,' chef droned. 'When he died in

1715 his stomach was three times the size of the average adult. Dinner for Louis at Versailles, the palace he built for himself, consisted of some twenty-odd plates to be served in four courses.'

A few grunts of acknowledgement came from the throng.

'Louis insisted that his noblemen and woman lived at Versailles so he could keep an eye on them and their manners. But the king had strange habits, particularly when it came to food and insisted that the equerry of the kitchen first tasted every dish that was served to him because he was afraid of being poisoned. They had no proper cutlery but used a trencher, a flat round bread on which they served the food. When they finished their meal they would dip the trencher into the sauce and eat it. He held up a computer printout of an image. From somewhere someone mumbled, 'Pita?'

Chef ignored the interruption. 'Maybe we can try this out in the kitchen before our Versailles dinner. He paused to pat Arafat and took from Mahmoud a second printed sheet. He put on a pair of reading glasses and expounded, 'French cuisine changed very little during the Middle Ages, it remained dominated by certain cereals for the poor and spicy boiled meats. Vegetables were generally considered indigestible. But during the reign of Louis all of that changed. Louis loved all fine things and certain delicacies. His love for his garden and the fruits and vegetables it produced set the stage for a culinary revolution so, what types of food would the kitchen have served to this gourmand, our King Louis?'

Chef answered his own question. '*Haute cuisine* was first linked to a French chef named La Varenne. He published the first true French cookbook. Chef puffed out his chest to emphasis the point he was making, 'His book makes the earliest known reference to *roux*, using pork fat.'

He bellowed the word *pork* and continued, 'La Varenne published a book on pastry in 1667, *Le Parfait Confiturier*; his recipes marked a change from the old style of French cooking to the new lighter dishes.

Ignoring the glazed looks of his audience he continued unabashedly, 'Mahmoud has found an authentic menu on the Internet. Here are some of the dishes. An *oille*, a stew of spiced duck or partridge and even pigeon; chickens cooked in embers, galantines, partridge and pigeon pies, *potage*, they loved potage. Here we have *potage à la jacobine*, a stew of chicken served in almond sauce over a layer of cheese. And they served fried sheep's testicles,' a murmur of appreciation was heard from the middle-eastern fraternity, 'and fish, oysters and salmon. Lots of peas, Louis had his kitchens import green peas from Italy and had them packed in rose leaves to keep them fresh. I hate to admit it, but Italy beat us to it at the *haute cuisine*. Interesting!'

He paused, reflecting on what he had told his troops. '*Très bien*, we have much to work with and we have yet to look at desserts.'

He patted Mahmoud on the head and added, 'With thanks to Mahmoud here who went to the Internet for the recipes and discovered that such a dinner has previously been held at the Palace Versailles.' He acknowledged that the eyes of his audience had glazed over and most seemed to be nearing a state of catatonia.

'*Dégage,*' he bellowed followed by a mumbled, '*Fils de pute.*'

Almost as a second thought he added, 'Chamber music will be played throughout, the dining room staff will wear the traditional long curly wigs and I will as closely as possible decorate the dining room like the anti-chamber of the *Grand Couvert*, where Louis himself dined. I believe he favored small orange trees in pots and green peas,' he whispered with a certain reverence.

It may have been the thought of long curly wigs, or maybe green peas, but chef had a sudden moment. He patted Mahmoud and Arafat on their heads and smiled. And in that moment chef decided to make something of this boy. As is the way with artists and dreamers, he closed his eyes and envisaged a future in his truffle orchard, a restaurant serving only classic French country recipes with Mahmoud in the kitchen as his *sous chef.*

As the galley staff began dispersing in response to his earlier order, chef held up his hand with the authority of a traffic warden. There was an audible gasp of horror at the prospect of the lecture on the Versailles dinner continuing but chef surprised them all with a segue to, 'I have made a change in the galley. I am promoting Mahmoud to a *commis*, a junior chef and he will report directly to me.'

No one except for his uncle and the chef had ever chosen Mahmoud for any special task. For the second time in his life he felt special. He felt chosen but was also conflicted. Was he chosen by chef to be better than the others in the galley or was he chosen by his uncle to rid the world of chef's pig. To do or not to do, that was the question.

Ahmed brushed past him on his way to the dishes. 'Teacher's pet,' he whispered into Mahmoud's ear. 'Don't let it stop you from doing Imam's will.'

25

Anyone For Hashish?

Major Barbara Cock had time on her hands and nothing to do. She entered the galley unannounced looking for the chef but found it empty but for Mahmoud seated at a computer at the far end of the galley with his back to her. Something about his demeanour worried her. The boy was strung like a tightrope, a sight she did not like to see in one so young. She approached him silently and kibitzed over his shoulder at the website open on his computer. All she saw was an empty screen. She had observed more cases of trauma in the very young than she cared to remember and here she had before her eyes a perfect candidate. She moved in close. She peered over his shoulder and whispered in his ear.

'What have we here?'

Mahmoud swivelled on his chair and paled.

Barbara patted him on the hand and pushed a lock of hair from his eyes. These two caring gestures from a stranger were all it took for Mahmoud to unload the pressures he was under to please two masters. His eyes crossed and he slumped to the side unconscious.

Barbara was familiar with the journey the boy was on, she had seen the symptoms in young soldiers ordered to act against their morals. She waited for the boy to come back from that wonderful nether land he had escaped to. She filed her nails as she waited. He opened his eyes and stared back at hers.

'Tell me about it' she said, and Mahmoud did exactly that.

Major Barbara answered to no master but herself. Her moral compass was her guide and she followed that star to the letter. She believed that certain people were evil and if she were asked to target them she felt no compunction about doing so. But much as she targeted evil she also believed in rewarding good.

As she listened to the Arab boy's dilemma it astonished her to think that he thought that any time he took a step wrong and did not do what his uncle the imam had asked of him – to kill the truffle pig – then the sky would fall in on him.

She had treated many men in combat who had fought to stay alive, who limped home damaged to get on with life, so to believe that failing to honour a fatwa on a truffle pig meant the end of all existence seemed to Major Barbara Cock to be totally idiotic.

How interesting, she reflected, that this village imam seemed to be the one to blame for chef's neurosis and this boy's dilemma, this imam who hated pigs and who did not seem too keen on his nephew either.

Perhaps this imam needed to be taught a lesson.

'Consider this,' she instructed Mahmoud and the small pig that never left his side, 'You could throw this little pig overboard and he would be eaten by the sharks, then go back to living with your uncle and then go to jail as chef will no doubt press charges and in return you will be rewarded in Paradise – wherever Paradise is because no-one has come back from there or made a video, not even Richard Branson or Michael Moore – or,' she continued, 'you can become a chef and one day own a restaurant of your own because you obviously have talent and chef seems keen to nurture it. It really seems a simple choice to make.'

Mahmoud had no idea what he would do with a dozen virgins if he had them; in fact, he had no idea of what he would do with only one. Paradise for him had always been an extra piece of meat in his auntie's very watery stew. And so it was that a glimmering of common sense took root in Mahmoud's head and like a vine began to grow.

But threats, like weeds, are not got rid of easily and while young Mahmoud and the major chewed the cud that sunny afternoon a sinister figure lurked unknown to them just out of earshot. Away from the watchful eye of chef, Ahmed the defrocked *sous chef* puffed away on his hookah in the freezer beside a side of beef. From his refuge in the freezer Ahmed could not be seen. And from his refuge in the freezer he watched and listened to the dialogue between the imam's nephew, Mahmoud, and the passenger known as Major Barbara Cock.

As some readers may be aware, the smoking of hashish can at times cloud one's comprehension but it was clear to Ahmed, judging from the body language of the major, that she was having a powerful effect on Mahmoud the young and impressionable minder of the chef's pig. For some time now Ahmed had felt the boy was starting to rethink his uncle's fatwa on the pig and all the work the imam had done to mold his nephew's thinking may literally go up in smoke. *How could the boy give up the promise of paradise for a job on board a cruise ship or learn how to cook the French way and forget his own Tunisian cuisine?*

To Ahmed nothing in this life compared with a dozen virgins even if they came on an instalment plan. *Perhaps it's up to me to toss that smelly piglet overboard.*

He puffed on the hookah and let the smoke dribble from his mouth. He would definitely get rid of the pig himself if young Mahmoud refused to do it.

But as is the way with unobserved observers, unobserved observers can often be observed. A small pig with pink-ringed eyes and a sensitive nature was also an observer and armed with an ample dose of intuition it took a sharp breath inward, a short and sudden intake of hashish.

One little known fact about a truffle pig is that it also has a set of quite sharp teeth. Arafat's gaze became focused on Ahmed's shoes and as he gazed at the battered loafers they turned into roots of a giant tree and the tree and the roots looked menacing. And as it gazed through shimmering vision at the roots the little pig observed that woven into these giant roots was a snake with bulging eyes. But it wasn't the snake or the roots that captured Arafat's attention, it was the trove of truffles waiting to be snuffled. The snake was rearing to protect the truffles. In an instant Arafat lunged forward and sunk her baby teeth into first one snake and then the other, into the ankles of Ahmed the deposed *sous chef*.

Ahmed's scream brought Mahmoud and the major running over. Ahmed and a side of beef lay entwined like lovers and very still. Arafat sat dazed and bewildered beside them then tottered unsteadily towards Mahmoud. The smell of hashish said it all. Mahmoud knew beyond a doubt that the little pig needed his protection.

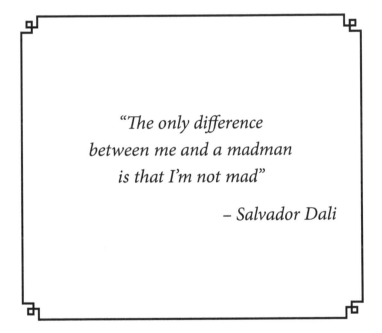

"*The only difference between me and a madman is that I'm not mad*"

– Salvador Dali

26

Fine Art

Dirk von Klimt was ready to score. The morning was clear and blue and the sea calm. Today at the auction he would show them, confuse them with art speak, target their greed and sell them a gamble that would never pay off. He released his mane of grey hair so that it fell to his shoulders.

'I am a beautiful man,' he said to his reflection in the mirror and kissed the diamond on his little finger.

He would make back his losses at the casino and like every slightly crooked art dealer he bargained on an ace in the pack. His ace was the genuine article, the painting that would stand up to scrutiny, and the work that would pass the test of the most astute of buyers. His masterpiece.

From his closet he withdrew a small painting of a white tree, an exquisite piece by a Japanese master. In his heart of hearts he knew that this small landscape, this Japanese tree, would do the trick.

When earlier that year he was called in to value the contents of an old lady's attic he found this gem hidden behind a stack of ugly landscapes. The old lady had no idea what it was worth, didn't even know that it was there but Dirk knew. Knew he had found a masterpiece in the old lady's attic, one that would increase his fortunes immensely. So he acquired the painting for next to nothing as part of a deal for the ugly landscapes. This work would sell for fifty thousand dollars and there could be even more on resale.

Even at a distance the white branches of the tree seemed illuminated by the light that the artist had brought to the landscape. Dirk would start the auction with the genuine article. Then all false works that followed would benefit.

Dirk stood resplendent in white, his white-grey hair spread Christ-like around his shoulders, the monocle lodged over his left eye glistening.

'And who will start the bidding at twenty thousand?'

The auditorium was packed with eager buyers, each holding a paddle on which was embossed their personal number.

'A true masterpiece and highly sought after by major collections,' Dirk crooned, his tensed knuckles stood white from holding tight on to the paddles. His voice oozed out like liquid caramel willing those paddles to rise. So involved was he with the sound of his voice that he failed to hear the squeaking of a Zimmer frame being shakily guided by his nemesis, Maurice, as he trundled down the central isle towards the empty seat at the end of a row. Resting across the handles of the Zimmer frame and balanced there by Maurice's pointed chin was a paddle displaying a number: eleven.

'Whomever buys this painting will double his money in two years, any museum will pay you more,' Dirk declared. 'Do I hear seventy-five thousand?'

In his peripheral vision Dirk made out the number 11 and swivelled. He could hardly believe his eyes. Maurice the accountant from Britain with the bottle-bottom glasses was holding up his paddle with one hand while the other steadied the Zimmer.

A large woman in a floral dress raised her paddle, another paddle flashed in the back right-hand corner of the room. The bidding was now at $90,000. Dirk smiled, his silver tooth laid bare. And then it happened. Paddle number 11 took the bidding to $100,000. There was an audible gasp from the audience and the other two bidders put down their paddles. This is it, Dirk conceded; the turd from the casino was the winning bidder. On last valuation the painting saw $50,000. He, Dirk von Klimt, had come out on top by $50,000.

He smothered a smile and continued with the auction. The audience, blood now hot for the chase, competed for the fakes before heading off to enjoy their purchases over a cup of tea and scones.

Goldfarb watched the proceedings with amusement. It came as a surprise to see the shrunken, bent figure of Maurice the bridge player register his name for a paddle and plod his way down to the front row clutching onto his Zimmer frame. And an even greater surprise to see the old man buy a painting for one hundred thousand dollars.

Goldfarb had played several rounds of blackjack with the bridge-playing widows Fanny and Ethel from San Francisco but there had been no sign of Maurice the bridge player in the ship's casino since that fateful day he beat the bank while the ship was berthed in St Tropez. Goldfarb reflected on his conversation with his partner, Brenda Willing, just that afternoon. She had hit a winning streak and she was on a roll, the company was good at Monaco's main casino and the cards loved her. If Goldfarb pulled his weight they would have enough in the kitty to pay out their lease by week's end and wave the dreadful landlady and her gruesome grandson goodbye. Goldfarb reckoned one good round of blackjack with the right opponent would see them through.

He watched the remaining passengers file out of the auditorium for their afternoon tea. Only Maurice remained and he was coming Goldfarb's way crab fashion supported by his Zimmer.

Goldfarb's artfully placed shoe blocked the frame's progress for which Goldfarb, a picture of mock regret, apologised. The old man looked at his reflection in Goldfarb's dark glasses and a knowing smile split his wrinkled face like a knife through a rotting apple.

27

A Creature Of The Night

On the top deck of the *Pacific Belle* beside and behind the lido area is a small and secluded space. It was into this space that chef released his truffle pig each evening at midnight. The reason he released his pig into this enclosure, bounded on three sides by a child's playpen, was so that his precious little pig could see the stars. For one hour each night, heavy sea excluded, Arafat could star-watch while the chef sweated toxins inside the crew's gymnasium on the lower deck.

As Arafat gazed at the Milky Way, watched over by a guiding star and an ageing albatross, another figure headed for the hallowed space, a gym mat under one arm. And while Arafat pondered the secrets of the universe the mysterious figure lay down upon his mat alongside him and did one hundred press-ups and several squats.

Then, like clockwork every single night, the figure rolled up his mat and walked away, with not a word to the small pink truffle pig. The repeated movements the man made as he lay out on the deck on his mat must be for a reason, the pig concluded. And even though Arafat snuffled about and made some snorting noises to attract the man's attention other than a casual pat on the head the mysterious stranger treated him with total indifference. There was nothing about the man's scent that the pig recognised. He didn't smell of galley, nor did he smell of truffle, nor of Mahmoud or chef or hashish or captain or sheikh or any member of the galley staff. It was a rather unpleasant scent hitherto unknown to Arafat, a scent she didn't particularly like, one that was slightly like the whiff chef exuded when a soufflé suddenly dropped – something somewhat unpleasant.

This presented a conundrum for a small and innocent animal. The dark and mysterious figure, a rolled-up mat under his arm, always left well before chef returned and well before any seaman appeared to do the nightly swabbing of the deck.

It was as though this mysterious creature of the night didn't want to be discovered. Discovered by anyone or anything.

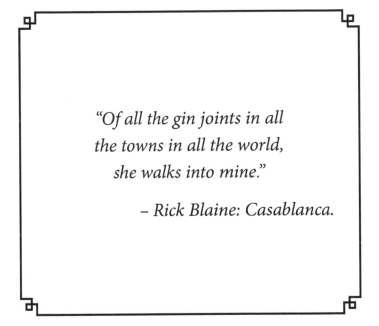

"Of all the gin joints in all the towns in all the world, she walks into mine."

– Rick Blaine: Casablanca.

28

Casablanca

The sheikh was only too happy for Sebastian to go off on his own. He had urged Sebastian to go but to avoid the casino at all costs and particularly Goldfarb the New York Jewish gambler with the dark glasses and the gold chains. The sheikh was saving that encounter for himself.

Late at night the Jazz Club was dim and empty. A black man dressed in a dinner suit was tinkling on the keys of a baby grand while a barman polished glasses. *All we need is Humphrey Bogart and Ingrid Bergman and this could be a scene from Casablanca,* Sebastian almost voiced aloud as he hugged an apple martini and waited for Pamela Lawson-Groves III to arrive. He adjusted his expression from the real sheikh's angry and dissatisfied look to one that was bland but interested and prepared his script. This was about romance. A dimly lit jazz club, a bored coloured tinkling on piano keys, a barman polishing glasses, a handsome but lonely sheikh waiting for the right woman to come into his life.

Make her eager. Pain, there must be some pain, he figured. *Factor in a love that could never be, ease the situation to be about a love that has a little chance of working, and then find a way around the difficulties.*

He grew excited as he mentally worked on this scenario, gently muttering to himself. If that chance meeting with the real sheikh had damaged his chances then this was his opportunity to repair any damage done. Music! He needed the correct music to create the mood, the film noir mood of the famous last scene in *Casablanca*.

Sebastian clicked his fingers at the piano player, 'Do you know *As Time Goes By?*'

It was late and the piano player, an African American from Georgia, who usually played the New Orleans jazz circuit, had smoked two joints and was high. Through heavy lids he cast a blazing bloodshot eye at the middle-eastern crazy alone at a table muttering and smiled in condescension, 'Of course, what piano player doesn't?'

It was well into the fifth rendition of *As Time Goes By* that Pamela cautiously poked her blonde head around the door of the Jazz Club and flashed a blinding smile at Sebastian. Sebastian fixed his bored but interested expression and stood to greet her. She appeared a little wary, as though not knowing how to react.

'You seemed so unfriendly when we met on deck this afternoon,' she shyly muttered through her smile.

He opened his eyes wide with astonishment and blinked rapidly, 'did we meet on deck? I think I was asleep this afternoon. It must have been my double that you met. This happens to me all the time.'

Pamela hid her relief behind a smile and visibly relaxed. *Of course! How silly.* It was the double she had met on deck that afternoon and not this charming, wealthy, handsome, super – cool sheikh.

He clicked his fingers at the barman and mouthed a request for, 'Two more apple martinis.'

Pamela edged a little closer and queried intimately, 'your double, is he a joker? He said he had four wives and five houses.'

The barman sidled over with two apple martinis and placed them on the table.

'He is an unusual chap, my double. He's good at impersonations. He was a professional actor, one of the best around, the star of his own TV show. I'm lucky to have him.'

He stopped himself from waxing too lyrical about his double and returned to the subject on hand.

'The fellow is scrupulously honest. He does have four wives that part is true, but as to owning five houses, I don't think so. They all live together under one roof. As for me, I am single, but when I meet the

CASABLANCA

right woman, one who understands me, then who knows, that could all change.'

Pamela gently laid her hand upon his arm and gazed intensely into his eyes. 'Honey,' she purred, 'this may surprise you but I am a toe reader.'

Sebastian hid his surprise with the skill of a trained actor. It was a remark completely out of left field. Why would a wealthy heiress with good legs and a chain of restaurants want or need to read toes, or any other part of a person's foot for that matter? He found the idea of studying other peoples' feet repugnant. Her obvious line of dialogue should be about her houses or her fast food restaurants. He segued politely away from the subject of feet and guided her back to the script as he envisaged it, 'Where is your favourite place to live or does it depend upon your business'?

She, however, was a woman of single-mindedness. 'You can learn a lot about a man from his big toe,' she crooned.

He attempted to remove himself from the under-the-table contact with her feet.

This sudden movement on his part seemed to relay his message. And with the intuition of a seasoned hunter she returned to his script.

'Washington is my home base, honey, but I go to Salt Lake in the winter to ski. Do they ski in the desert?'

He shook his head. 'You rarely see snow in the desert,' he assured her and decided that perhaps she wasn't the brightest kid on the block.

'I don't want to be pushy but maybe you could visit me in Washington one day?'

* * *

As can so often happen fate will reach in and disturb the best thought out scenario. At this highpoint of the conversation, when at last it seemed he was making progress with this blonde woman with good legs and a chain of fast food restaurants, a woman who represented a future free of playing double to a bullying sheikh, Sebastian's cell phone rang. He was left with no choice but to take the call.

He nodded a polite apology to Pamela and edged away for privacy.

The dulcet tones of his employer blasted in his ear, 'Where the fuck are you? I'm sweating like a camel's hump at an oasis. The air conditioning won't work and the asshole of a butler doesn't answer the buzzer.'

Sebastian assumed a look of one charged with enormous responsibility and made his excuses to Pamela. A business call he must take in his suite, his double had alerted him. But, he assured her, they must meet again and, yes, he would love to visit Washington sometime in the future. As he was about to disappear through the door of the bar he turned and quoted the final words from *Casablanca*, those famous lines that had stimulated star-crossed lovers across the generations: 'I think this is the beginning of a beautiful friendship.' Then, with a theatrical flourish, he disappeared in a billow of white.

Pamela sipped her martini and basked in the moment, revelling in this brief but charming meeting with her sheikh, the sheikh so different from his double and so charming. She knew she would like to know him better. After all, she reasoned, her Washington home was much too large to live in alone. What she needed was a man in her life who could help her run her restaurants. She had always wanted a house somewhere in a desert, she mused; perhaps they could use his as a holiday home. What was it that the sheikh had said as he turned to say goodbye? 'I think this is the beginning of a beautiful friendship'

Did he mean it? She wondered.

Unfortunately for Sebastian, subtlety was lost on the widow from Washington. The only Casablanca Pamela knew of was a type of window covering. 'Can you play *Mamma Mia?*' she smiled at the pianist as he rattled off the umpteenth version of *As Time Goes By*.

Shame about the piano player, Pamela reflected, *he only seems to know one song and that was becoming tedious.*

29

Holy Moley

Sheikh Hasim represented many things to many people but to his accountant Habibi he represented bread and butter. The sheikh was a man with an eye for the ladies but had no eye at all for business. As one of the old sheikh's family, income was never ending and what to do with it an ongoing problem.

A chance meeting with a financial adviser, a Pakistani named Habibi, at an investment bank in Mayfair led to a lasting mutually beneficial arrangement. Back in England Habibi owned a modest semi, a spotty Pakistani wife plus an elderly bedridden mother. He still got his medicines on national health and claimed a pension for his mother. But after meeting Hasim he waved Britannia goodbye and settled for a better life in the Middle East.

The partnership was profitable for both. Habibi made the investment decisions and ran the office for his employer, Sheikh Hasim, who spent the profits. In return for making the sheikh richer, Habibi had a house and servants and a generous income in the Emirates.

Part of this new found good fortune was a nail technician from Manchester named Blanche with an hourglass figure and legs up to her armpits. Habibi had fortuned upon Blanche when a hangnail hung in the way of his counting piles of banknotes for the sheikh. Blanche was nineteen and hungry. She wanted to see the world and this small round very black Pakistani was her pathway to paradise.

But Habibi found that this child bride with a body like young Bardot did nothing for his sense of security. To keep Blanche safe from competition he took her everywhere with him. His other worry was the sheikh himself who had a reputation of absconding with other men's wives when the fancy took him.

Had things been otherwise Blanche would never have met Sebastian, the rather handsome actor now housed under her roof undergoing physical changes before her very eyes. From her vantage point at the other end of a very large house overlooking the Arabian Sea, Blanche watched at first with curiosity and then with horror as this handsome, sexy actor transformed much like a monarch in reverse from a butterfly back to a caterpillar.

Her glitzy persona housed a fragile and romantic heart, which as each bandage was unravelled, shattered just a little and gradually crumbled as she watched the handsome young actor get uglier, a sculpted ski jump nose turn bulbous, kissable lips turn puce and a muscular body loose definition and gain flab. And then there was the mole. Some moles are seen to be attractive. Sometime in the '30s women took to penciling them on as beauty spots but the mole that occupied the nose of Sheikh Hasim fell more into the category of 'warty lump.' It was large, black and cratered and looked rather like a miniature volcano. It was the mole that made Blanche break her silence and it was kippers for breakfast that provided opportunity.

Habibi had been an Englishman long enough to be acquainted with some quaint local habits. Some may choose to run around a park to start the day but for Habibi it was kippers. One morning, as Habibi focused on filleting his kipper, Blanche slid out from under his radar. She took advantage of him picking bones to see Sebastian alone and caution him. Once up close and personal she was horrified to discover that the once-handsome actor was now a mirror image of Habibi's boss, the sheikh. Devastated, she begged Sebastian not to make any further changes and while Habibi dodged the bones in his kipper she laboured on top of the sheikh's English double. When their mutual desire was satisfied and they shared Sebastian's pillow it was then that Blanche produced her masterpiece, a false mole, and a mole that could be fixed and removed when necessary. She had learned many useful things as a nail technician and creating a false mole from acrylic and knowing how to stick it on was just one example.

While she and Sebastian shared a cigarette she showed him the art of false mole attachment. Beware of overheating, she cautioned, this material is highly flammable and heat will tend to melt the adhesive. The new sculpted mole was identical to the sheikh's even down to the colour and shape and it was this mole that they named 'Bubby' that came to represent their special secret. Thereafter and for all time there was a mole in Sheikh Hasim's service, a mole called Bubby that would eventually be his downfall.

As time passed and Sebastian fell into his role as a double, Blanche's passion for the English actor faded and if it weren't for the three-carat diamond earrings she wanted for her birthday, the acrylic mole might forever have remained a secret. The three-carat diamonds, one to each ear, were the catalyst for Blanche's change of heart. As simple a girl as Blanche appeared, she knew on which side her bread was buttered. Small, round Pakistanis were not thick on the ground, particularly those who held her in esteem. So as she admired the glittering gems nestled in their bed of satin and gratefully hugged Habibi she felt a pang of conscience about her deception and immediately decided to come clean. Come clean about the acrylic mole she had modelled for the double.

Habibi decided not to pursue Blanche's motives. He was more concerned with keeping Blanche than keeping the double's secret. He added a note to Sebastian's file on his computer, a note that simply stated that a mole on his nose could under certain circumstances detach and that all care should be taken to prevent it.

30

Ajaccio

Chef prepared to go to market. From the deck of the *Pacific Belle* he observed his favourite port of call as the red tiled roofs and church spires of Ajaccio emerged through the early morning mist. He loved the sea-facing promenade lined with palm trees and cafes. Ajaccio, the main port of Corsica, where Napoleon took his first breath, where he played as a child, where the temperature remains mild throughout the year and where chef felt sure he would find the small potted orange trees and the long curly wigs he needed to give his Versailles dinner authenticity.

The wooded mountains surrounding the town loomed like guardians through the mist but it was a mist that held the promise of blue skies and even bluer waters and any feelings of gloom the chef may have had about his present or his future melted away in the beauty of the moment.

As much as he wanted to go ashore with Arafat he knew that the little pig would restrict his entry into the central market place. He would be first to disembark so would miss the hordes of tourists and with a little luck would be back on board in time for lunch and Arafat would barely miss him.

She had become as much attached to Mahmoud as she was to the chef. So as the mooring ropes were fixed and the disembarkation gangway put in place chef showed his identification papers to the petty officer and headed for the centre of Ajaccio based around the sixteenth-century citadel and spreading west and north of the citadel into town. He walked the narrow cobbled streets of the Old Town towards *Place Marechal Foch*. He passed pastel painted houses and saw the landmark house where Bonaparte was born, now the National Bonaparte Museum. Signposts pointed to the caves in which the great man played, the streets and places bearing his name and the statues in his memory. It was a living monument to the little general.

Chef headed to where he hoped to find the fruit trees, peas, roses and foodstuffs necessary for his Versailles dinner. The smell of fresh ground coffee wafted out from the street cafes and chef felt a bubble of something that resembled joy fighting to free itself within his chest. He could not resist stopping for a coffee and a chestnut tart, a specialty of the region, and to feel the sunlight on his face and the soft temperate breezes whistle around his ears. It was no wonder that his fellow Frenchmen escaped the harshness of a Parisian winter to holiday on this beautiful island.

And it was while chef turned his face to the sunlight and closed his eyes to imagine for a moment that he felt the tingle of clear blue Mediterranean waters playing around his bare toes that he had a revelation. He would devise an extraordinary dessert as the *pièce de résistance* of the Versailles dinner; an individual dessert, one to each, no questions asked, as the ending to a perfect meal.

And while chef wiggled his toes in an imaginary clear blue pool and dreamt of force-feeding diet-conscious passengers a high calorie dessert Arafat, his small truffle pig, was facing the biggest threat to her existence.

31

Ahmed and Aspic

While Chef Armand stood up on deck admiring the spires of Ajaccio, Mahmoud paced the galley thinking about aspic. *Mind my pig and make up the aspic* had been the chef's final words to Mahmoud as he headed for shore.

The newly appointed junior chef approached this task like David did Goliath. But one thing he knew for certain, was that he was no multi-tasker and early in the morning a small truffle pig named Arafat demanded his attention.

He was aware that on the top deck of the *Pacific Belle*, just beside and behind the lido area was a small and secluded space quite hidden from the passengers and crew. He knew that each evening into this space chef released his truffle pig. The reason chef released the pig into this enclosure, bounded on three sides by a child's playpen was so that his precious truffle pig could gaze at the stars. In a vaguely logical way, Mahmoud could therefore see the benefits of Arafat getting sunlight and a whiff of early morning air while he, the new assistant chef, struggled to prepare an aspic that would make chef smile.

Leash in hand, with truffle piglet Arafat trotting alongside, he headed for the lido through a ship still half asleep.

As passengers glanced through bleary eyes at watches, checked tour tickets for departure times and thankfully rolled over in their beds, the ageing albatross, forever on the lookout for diversity, sat high on the yardarm and watched as a small and swarthy boy came up on deck with a small pink pig on a leash and made their way to the playpen on the lido deck.

Always keen to leave his mark on a less than perfect world the albatross stretched his wing and if one could countenance relish on an albatross, he released his digested breakfast on to the lido deck then with a certain satisfaction pecked a mite from beneath his wing feathers.

The boy led the pig into the playpen and beside it placed a bowl of freshly scrambled eggs. After a quick pat to the small pig's head Mahmoud headed down the stairwell and disappeared.

And all the while inside his head Mahmoud heard the voice of Chef Armand, a voice that repeated and repeated, *Make sure that the gelatin melts, no lumps, remember no lumps and then you add it to the broth, never before, never before, and then you add the wine, never before, never before, remember, remember, no lumps, then you refrigerate.*

And as is the case when one is preoccupied, Mahmoud, the newly appointed chef's assistant, failed to notice the figure that shadowed him and came to rest behind the galley door.

As Mahmoud reached for the pots and the wooden spoons and flicked on the gas jets that powered the burners, broke up the gelatin and measured out the broth and wine, deposed *sous chef* Ahmed, a spy for Mahmoud's uncle the imam, knew what he had to do.

The instant chef had announced to one and all that Mahmoud was to become his favoured assistant Ahmed saw the writing on the wall. The boy lacked the character and the belief to resist such an offer. He would never now harm chef's pampered truffle pig. It would be up to him, Ahmed, to get rid of the pig. He had known it as he rolled out his prayer mat at dawn's first light; he, Ahmed was the true believer, he would get rid of the pig for the imam, besides which the promise of several virgins was not an offer to be sneezed at.

This was his ideal opportunity. While Mahmoud flitted around making aspic and chef was on shore doing marketing, while the galley staff were in their bunks or performing their morning ablutions, now while the little pig was vulnerable and alone up there on the deck, now he could perform his jihad.

His plan of operation was a simple one. Holding an iron skillet and a piece of rope he headed for the lido deck. The rope was to tie the skillet to the pig so that when Ahmed tossed the pig overboard the weight of the skillet would weight it down and drown it.

Unaware that she was under siege and despite caws of resentment from the albatross above her head, Arafat demolished her scrambled eggs. She was about to tackle the blob of bird droppings when the arrival of Ahmed made her think more food was on the way and she waved her curly tail in a pig's joyous greeting.

As Ahmed boldly made his way across the lido deck another figure appeared at the top of the stairs, a small lithe figure in a tracksuit with a rolled-up exercise mat under each arm.

That small truffle pigs can squeal with the best of them was something Ahmed was well aware of and the memory of Arafat's small sharp teeth embedded in his ankle during the awful freezer incident was still painfully real. The only way to subdue this little animal, Ahmed figured, was to first knock it out with the skillet to stifle the din.

Cautiously he leaned close to the playpen and through the bars he offered a large and luscious piece of a sachertorte, freshly made by the pastry cook the previous evening. In his other hand he held the iron skillet ready to bring it down on the piglet's head. But as the piglet opened her small mouth to grab the chocolate cake a mighty blast from giant wings knocked her sideways and the ageing albatross, not to be outdone by a small truffle pig, swooped down and grabbed the sachertorte in its beak then soared heavenward.

With the skillet held high above his head and ready to strike, Ahmed, struggled to regain his balance and tottered forward to find a startled Arafat was sheltering in a corner of the playpen and out of reach.

Ahmed placed the skillet down on the deck and pondered. Fortunately he had carried more of the cake up on deck so he placed another larger portion inside the playpen to lure the pig close enough for Ahmed to protect it from another raid by the albatross.

Arafat's snout twitched. Tempted by the smell of the sachertorte she cautiously edged closer. She slunk towards the cake on her tummy until she was close enough to it to nuzzle it with her snout Ahmed slowly reached for the skillet without taking his eye off the piglet. But it seemed to have moved. He turned to look for it but someone had beaten him to it.

And as he turned to look for the skillet a slight figure in a tracksuit raised a hand holding the iron pan and brought it crashing down on Ahmed's vulnerable skull. He slid to the deck like an unevenly packed sack of spuds. The figure in the tracksuit tied the skillet to Ahmed's ankle, and grabbing him by the ankles lugged him towards the ship's rail. There was a dull splash as he forced Ahmed through the rails and into the water.

The mysterious figure in the tracksuit patted the small pink pig on the head, stood for a moment watching it slurp up the remainder of the sachertorte then casually picked up the rolled exercise mats and left without a backward glance.

*"I'm not crazy about reality,
but it's still the only place
to get a decent meal"*

– Groucho Marx.

32

Flambé

When Chef Armand eventually returned, weary from a market day, it was to find Arafat his truffle pig safely secured below decks, a moustache of ganache above her small pink snout, and fresh aspic in the refrigerator.

His shopping trip had been successful. He had found long curly wigs for his serving staff in a costume shop and potted orange trees in a plant nursery. All the produce necessary for this special dinner he had secured in the market – fresh fish, shellfish, poultry and even pigeons. True, he had exceeded his budget but this would be the first and the finest Versailles dinner ever held on board; he, Chef Armand, would see to that.

He dipped a finger into the aspic prepared by new assistant Mahmoud and smiled. It was as smooth as silk. He knew how to pick them. The boy was a natural.

Only when a review of crew was taken days later was it noted that a certain member of the galley staff, one Ahmed Mohammed Dhjou, had not returned from a supposed shore trip in Ajaccio, Corsica. Such things happened on cruise ships and the local police were duly notified. Ahmed's disappearance passed silently by, soon to be forgotten by all but one frustrated imam.

Night fell with a jolt and the *Pacific Belle* gathered her anchor like a woman her ball gown and prepared to make her departure. As she glided slowly from the quay and out to sea up on the hill the little Emperor Napoleon, forever cast in bronze, reflected on the trail of money the tourist swarms had joyfully left behind and he smiled along with the members of the local council.

The *Pacific Belle* gathered speed and wove among the tapestry of billowing waves and frothing foam as night embraced her weary passengers. They had retreated to the calm of their cabins, home from their frolicking on land and smug in the belief that their knowledge of the world had been expanded. And each, once safely tucked away surrounded by their treasures, languished in thoughts about the present or the past or the future.

As Major Barbara Cock agonised over which sheikh was which and the widowed sisters Ethel and Fanny lusted after a male flamenco dancer on the in-house movies; as Pushkin Goldfarb totted up his winnings at the blackjack table and wondered where his lover Brenda

Willing spent the night; as art dealer Dirk von Klimt surfed the internet for impoverished Haitian artists; as Sebastian practiced forging the sheikh's signature and Pamela Lawson-Groves III of the glistening white teeth sat silent, two trays of bleach whitening her uppers and her lowers, so did Armand the chef labour over a menu for his Versailles dinner. As he jotted down notes he sucked at the tip of his lead pencil, oblivious to health hazards and mumbling as he scribbled, *Les hors d'oeuvre; a royal ballotine of pheasant with truffle – 'Don't forget to mention health benefits of truffle on official menu'; petit pâté en croûte a la truffle; the tasty soft shell crabs he found at the market, 'Perfect'; crab aspic with truffle chaudfroid; a potage … a potage of duck; a soup, a pureed chestnut with truffles, and a bisque and fried sheep's testicles – 'a court favourite according to research.'*

The thought of sheep's testicles brought a rippling smile to his dimpled pink cheeks rather like a bad facelift in a strong wind as he wondered if Sheikh Hasim would take this item personally.

Naturally, he mused, he would not use real sheep's balls, rather a mix of chicken livers, or perhaps an oyster and seafood blend in choux pastry, made from lard of course to keep it fluffy, lard made from pig's fat. At the thought of using pig fat he sniggered once again.

As his mind created so did his pencil fly. *Les rots, Oille, wild pigeon, hare stew, wild salmon, roast beef, and game pie – use lard.*

And then it came to him. His *tour de force*, the perfect ending to a perfect meal that would be a talking point for years to come will be a *flambé*. A surge of energy burst through him and he jumped to his feet, eager to create his masterpiece, only to remember the galley staff was busy preparing dinner. It would be his creation, *flambé a la chef*.

Perhaps he would write a recipe book, he mused; he had many recipes to include. Perhaps that nice travel writer lady could help. It surprised him how often she entered his thoughts since she offered him some of her small pink pills. For a moment he saw her in his truffle orchard, a large straw hat upon her head. But he blinked away the image, shocked at how at that moment his heart beat faster. Maybe, he reflected, maybe some time he would ask her to visit—and as this idea took hold so did his temperature rise until he doused the rising flames of desire with a segue back to a *flambé*.

* * *

Below decks as the ship slipped gracefully through the rolling waves Captain Svensen, relishing his solitude, rejoiced as he read the contents of a fax received that afternoon from management. Its contents would certainly eliminate his problem.

The fax detailed complaints received from two guest lecturers, Rbib Dji of Mumbai and Simon

Schmitz of California, about the menu during the so called 'wellness' cruise and a note from the union rep complaining about the pig the chef kept in the galley, situations unacceptable to management. A replacement, three-star Michelin chef, Horst Schitz, a German, would be signing on in Marseilles on a three-month contract.

The fax went on to offer Chef Armand three months' long-service leave with an option to renew provided that when he signed on again he did so without his pig.

Ever since the voyage began the captain had been fielding complaints about the chef, complaints from Jerome the *maître d'* and from the ship's doctor, who was overburdened by multiple cases of irritable bowel. As much as chef's standards were admirable it would be good to work with an executive chef who was a team player.

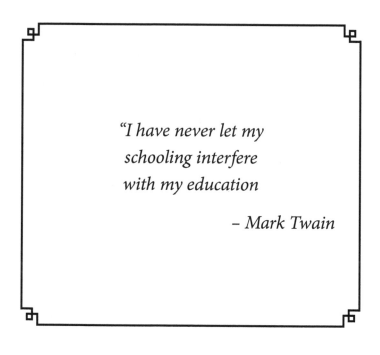

"*I have never let my schooling interfere with my education*

– *Mark Twain*

33

A Good Education

Though most of his clan went up to Oxford to read the classics Sheikh Hasim went up to read porn. His days at Oxford, underwritten by his father, consisted mostly of smoking a bong and reading girlie magazines. Not that his time amid the hallowed walls of the establishment was wasted, it polished off his rougher edges and gave him an accent passable with the upper classes. But any interest in European history or education generally dissipated and a day in Corsica steeped in the history of Napoleon held no allure for him at all. Left to his own devices the Sheikh took to his cabin to spend a day in bed to gather energy before returning to wives all wanting his attentions. His double, Sebastian, less worldly than the Sheikh, had joined a bus tour of the island and would be away all day.

So Sheikh Hasim was languishing in his bed scanning *The Tropic of Cancer* for good bits when the phone rang and the velvet voice of Habibi his accountant surfed the airways. Habibi rarely bothered Sheikh Hasim with business matters but lately things had got somewhat out of hand. Animal rights groups were causing mayhem for the Sheikh's shawarma fast food chain by holding up the delivery of live sheep needed to keep the fast food chain in business.

And as well as the problem with the animal activists Habibi had another reason to call. Only that day a threatening email had arrived in his inbox, an email with an illustration. The illustration took the form of a dagger run through a pile of round black bits that resembled sheep droppings. The meaning of this strange and badly illustrated email was open to interpretation but to Habibi its meaning was clear, the dagger was a threat and the pile of droppings must refer to Sheikh Hasim. The sheikh had remarkably little knowledge of his own business affairs so it came as some surprise for him to learn from Habibi that he was involved in importing live sheep.

'Why is it necessary to import sheep from other countries?' he innocently enquired.

Habibi, a non-practicing Muslim and not wishing to offend, nor lose a hand or foot, avoided mentioning that certain authorities insisted that sheep be imported live so that they could supervise their ritual slaughter, responded discreetly, 'Because we have no grass and sheep need grass.'

Hasim rarely showed a glimmering of business acumen but lounging as he was in his pajamas with nothing else to occupy his mind it seemed the time and place to make suggestions.

'Surely,' he surmised, 'if we had home grown sheep it would keep our costs down, and if we had grass we would have home grown sheep.'

It dawned on Habibi the error of his ways in calling the sheikh at all and rather than mentioning that in some places deserts were being converted to arable land through clever use of irrigation he chose to remain silent.

This unusual burst of cerebral energy sucked the lifeblood out of Sheikh Hasim and he fell back on to his pillows exhausted. The effort of moving a concept to another level was to his untaxed brain much like building a dam across the Yangtze.

This, he realised, must be the reason he found business and money so tiresome and boring, it was far too exhausting to think about.

He felt a sudden rush of anger at being interrupted on his day of rest for matters he could not control and all for a few stupid sheep and before Habibi could utter a word about the illustration he bellowed, 'You handle it, Habibi,' and the line went dead.

34

Gender Specific

Jerome the *maître d'* on the *Pacific Belle* was from humble beginnings. The only home he knew until the age of twelve was his parents' fish and chip shop, or The Chippery as he later called it. As early as he could remember Jerome had a thing for the Queen and as far back again her picture hung above the shop's deep fryer. The years had splattered her majesty with oil but still her steadfast gaze followed the boy Jerome as he helped his mum and dad, helped them wrap fish and chips and collect the money. So strong was her majesty's influence that his burning passion was to serve her at a palace, Buckingham or Windsor it mattered not to him. He was always somewhat of an elite; hated vulgarity and nasty body odours, and in his dreams he saw himself as one of the better sorts.

Jerome found his accent, as an East End boy was a barrier to achieving this dream so he reinvented himself by taking elocution lessons. Putting on airs held no water with his parents, Sid and Doris, and soon they began giving him sideways glances. But he was a young man on a mission and he retreated into a chrysalis from which he later emerged as a suave and accomplished speaker of the Queen's English, wearing suits with knife-edged trousers and impeccable hair and nails.

So distressing was this transformation for his humble parents that Jerome left home and went to butler school where he learned housekeeping procedures for butlers and married a Sloane Ranger named Sarah. All attempts to acquire a posting in the royal household failed but Jerome eventually rose in the ranks of Harrods to become a food hall manager. A disillusioned Sarah, her dreams of rubbing shoulders with the royals shattered, took their children, his credit cards and deeds to the house and left Jerome with no option but to run away to sea where, elevated to the role of *maître d'*, his many talents could eventually find a home.

Jerome had never had an issue with his gender – he was a man who identified as such – but as he strolled between the rows of waiters dressed in costume and ready for the Versailles dinner it became apparent that most of his staff were rather more complicated than himself.

Give a man a stage and who knows what can happen. It could have been the grey curly wigs, the slathers of powder, the heavy rouge and lipstick that did it, but do the trick it did. The pomp of the court of Louis XIV affected Jerome's army of white shirted, black trousered conservative waiters alarmingly.

Jerome had recently seen a survey taken on a campus. The survey questioned the common belief that current acronyms used to describe expanded gender identities, LGBT or LGBTIG, did not cover all the categories required, a list of thirty-three in total. Those not covered by the current acronyms were transgenders, trans-persons, trans-men and trans-women, FTM (meaning female to male) or FTM (meaning transgender female), demi-boys, demi-girls and a-genders, inter-genders, inter-sexes and polygender, omnigender, bigender and androgene, non-binary, gender-non-confirming and gender fluid as well as cis-gender, that rare person who identifies with the gender of which they were born. Just to name a few.

And as he strolled along the costumed waiting staff, this normally conservative bunch of waiters and waitresses, he had to wonder into which of these gender identities many of them belonged. A normally masculine waiter from Bulgaria, not content with wig and make-up, added a string of pearls and earrings to his costume while three others were forced to remove their padded bras. A waitress from Manchester in pantaloons had added a substantial codpiece that couldn't help but catch the eye.

One more mature waiter with a marked squint had put on long false lashes, long enough to greatly obscure his vision, while a short apprentice stood unsteadily in red Manolo Blahniks. He, too, was considered a safety risk by Jerome and sent back to his cabin for a change of shoes. Playing dress-ups for the Versailles dinner had turned into a drag fest, which in a way had let the cat out of the bag.

As Jerome would later put it in terms of an excuse, 'They all got a bit carried away.'

While the waiting staff put the final touches to their make-up the passengers also caught the fever of the masked dinner. Butlers dropped off ornate masks to suites. Fine stockings were eased on to waxed legs; make-up applied to exfoliated cheeks and formal gowns were released from captivity.

Butlers scurried from laundry to suite with freshly steamed dinner jackets or newly polished brogues, tripping as they went on their tailcoats. Room service staff swanned back and forth with bottles of Mumm iced and ready. In the spa, the more adventurous were coiffured by the hairdressers or had purchased wigs ashore.

The mood of the galley was at fever pitch. Executive Chef Armand scurried from one workstation to another inspecting food preparation. The galley staff worked in a frenzy of activity. Copper pans and iron pots vied for space on the stovetops and the vapour swirled upward and around the faces of the sweating chefs. As Armand scurried from one work station to another, swearing in French at some and fondly patting others, truffle pig Arafat sat quietly in her basket observing the pandemonium through half-closed pink-rimmed eyes with all the calm of Buddha.

And unbeknown to chef, Major Barbara Cock, curious to check on her ward the Arab boy Mahmoud, took a cautious peek inside the galley. The scene she encountered took her breath away. She had witnessed many a parade ground in her time and lived in a home run by a general but seeing the chef controlling his staff was like the finest of military operations. *Why, he's just like daddy* she observed and felt a sudden pang, a pang she had not felt for quite some time and one that felt quite pleasant.

One must not underestimate this chef, she mused, *he may not play the game by all the rules but he certainly knows his business.*

Mahmoud, the chef's new assistant, seemed wrapped in a world of his own. He stood alongside the *pâtissier* watching with intensity as the Thai chef crafted the executive chef's *pièce de résistance*, his precious *flambé*.

In his cabin, Goldfarb sipped a glass of Mumm and counted his takings so far and admitted that catching a bridge cruise had turned out to be his lucky break. Not only had he converted several bridge players to the game of blackjack but in the process had also converted his winnings into an escape from his lease. One final match that was a case of honour would be with Sheikh Hasim. *Watch him though, he's tricky*, he heard the voice of Minchal his long-departed mother advise as she broke through his subconscious to issue yet another warning in his ear; *You could lose the lot.*

An invitation to join the captain's table for the big event had been slipped beneath his cabin door. Twice in one voyage as a guest of the captain could not be ignored. The only trouble was that if he shared a table with the two Saudi sheikhs another game of blackjack could not be avoided. Goldfarb decided that the subject must be dodged at any given moment. With one more day to go on board this ship he was taking no chances.

Maurice the accountant from London had been nowhere near the casino since the night he beat them all and Goldfarb assumed this was because his money had all been spent on the remarkable painting he had bought at auction. He too was someone that Goldfarb intended to steer clear of, particularly in the casino.

Goldfarb had Skyped Brenda as she was about to head off to a game. Brenda Willing, delicious in red, heading off to the local casino. Her luck had been holding and funnily enough most of the punters she had pitched against were off the local cruise ships.

Like a killer whale downing krill Brenda had made a meal of inexperienced and vulnerable punters. All was well. Their combined winnings would do the trick and Brenda was already looking at other apartments in their immediate seafront area.

35

Just Desserts

The captain's table sat square in the centre of the main dining room surrounded by silver candelabra. Captain Svensen was already seated there, ramrod straight and thinly disguised by an ornamental mask. He wondered as he observed his waiting staff decked out in wigs and livery, faces powdered and lips red, if the offer he made to chef of a Versailles dinner hadn't been an act of folly.

As the masked and glittering passengers filed into the dining room, waiters lit the candles on the many candelabra. In one corner, a group of singers quietly mouthed a madrigal to the gentle tinkling of a lute.

First to arrive at the captain's table were the guest lecturers the Indian yoga Rbib Dji in a white dhoti, dark skin goose-pimpled from the air conditioning, his mask apparent and his teeth not and his associate wellness lecturer Simon Schmitz resplendent in tuxedo, his long grey hair caught up in a stars and stripes bow, his large capped teeth as even and white as tombstones at Arlington. They nodded condescendingly, identified their places at the table and sat down leaving one seat between them.

The sheikh and his double, Sebastian, preceded the American woman Pamela Lawson-Groves III by minutes and a shuffle to avoid her ensued between the sheikh until finally Pamela found her seat between the food gurus, a signal that the sheikhs could relax and settle down. As pleasantries were exchanged Major Barbara Cock arrived in a gown embellished with what resembled epaulettes followed closely by the gambler Pushkin Goldfarb, a mask mounted over his trademark dark glasses. Fortunately for Major Barbara she was seated opposite the sheikh and his double. She realised this might well be her last opportunity to identify her target. No further instructions had come from her client, the man with the dog on the island. She sensed the captain's level of anxiety and nodded him a greeting to which he nodded back.

The woman had been a godsend. Since the major had calmed Chef Armand's savage breast all had gone quiet in the galley and in the dining room. A word in their ear about commission on book sales and the guest lecturers backed off from trying to influence chef and other than an outbreak of irritable bowel syndrome among the more diet conscious everything on board ship was relatively calm.

Once the night was over Captain Svensen would gently but firmly wish this executive chef farewell and if he …

He was woken from his reverie by a trumpet call as Chef Armand in wig and gaiters strutted into the dining-room bound for the captain's table, followed by a trail of waiters, suitably attired and carrying massive platters of food.

As they branched off to other tables to deposit the platters the chef continued to the captain's table followed by a waiter with a tray on which was a boar's head, eye sockets filled with a collage of green olives while wearing a frilly collar and what looked like an Arab headdress.

With a flourish of a lace hanky, chef indicated the space directly in front of the sheikh and his double and there the waiter placed the boar's head, unblinkingly staring directly at them. Captain Svensen turned pale. Powerless to do a thing he sat there. *Dismissing this chef cannot come a minute too soon. This could be the end of bookings from the Saudis.*

With a flourish of his lace hanky chef backed away theatrically from the table and strutted back to the kitchen. Barbara could swear he winked at her and she had to admire his attitude. She was not one for poncey men but being poncey suited Chef Armand. She caught the glance of the captain and her heart went out to him, the poor man was blinking anxiously behind his mask.

One sheikh, if colour was any indication of who was real and who was not, had turned a shade of puce. Too slim evidence on which to base her findings, Barbara thought, and mouthed a silent prayer that somehow, this night, her target would be revealed.

The bewigged waiters delivered course after course of food and as the guests imbibed and indulged their chatter rose in volume. Only the boar's head was silent, the collage of green olives where its eyes should be staring blankly at the world at large.

The waiting staff grew scruffier as the night progressed and Barbara wondered if some secret tippling was happening behind the scenes. Wigs had begun to slip and one waiter appeared in a pair of high heel shoes. You could say, she thought, that the party was getting rougher the longer the evening wore on. But something was about to happen that would prove to be her *coup de grâce.*'

Soups and stuffed pigeon, stews, roasted meats, fish and fowl, sweetbreads and sheep's testicles and a very strange mixture made of pigeon eggs and mandarin pieces were served to the table on loaded platters and tureens while all the while yoga Rbib Dji, oblivious to the mountains of food, ate quietly from a drawstring bag, munching contentedly on a mixture of nuts, raw carrots, quinoa and kale like a horse from a chaff bag while his neighbour, the attractive thrice-married – bridge-playing Pamela Lawson-Groves III handed out her business cards and argued with her health conscious neighbours as to the benefits to body and soul of Southern Fried Chicken.

The lute player strummed a chord and the lights dimmed. A hush of expectancy fell like a curtain over the passengers. Something special was about to happen.

The waiters, wigs flying, came trotting in like the running of the bulls at Pamplona, carrying trays of exotic desserts. Behind them came Chef Armand in full Louis regalia leading his pet pig Arafat on a leash. The dessert, a bombe Alaska, the meringue in petals of softest pink like roses about to bloom was topped by ornamental spun sugar in the shape of the Eiffel Tower that twinkled like fireflies in the candlelight.

As chef strutted among the tables waving a lace hanky the French national anthem blared through the sound system and waiters deposited a dessert before each guest, starting with the captain's table. Waiters worked in tandem decanting heated spirits on to the bombe before gently touching it with a lighted taper. One by one the desserts ignited like fireworks in a blaze of light and colour.

The waiter behind Sebastian poured heated brandy on to the bombe while another touched it with a taper. Being curious of nature and an inveterate sniffer, Sebastian pushed back his white keffiyeh and leant forward over the dessert to sniff it at precisely the moment that the taper hit the sauce. As the flames leapt Sebastian rapidly removed his face. But his reaction came seconds too late and the inevitable happened. The adhesive fixing his acrylic mole to his nose melted and began to ooze slowly down towards his dessert like molten lava, carrying the mole with it.

Adhesive and mole plopped gently into the melted meringue and the half-submerged Eiffel Tower. It was at this precise moment that Major Barbara Cock, with spoon poised to attack her bombe Alaska, looked up and saw, much like watching the ball descend at midnight in Time Square, the large brown warty mole fall. Later she thought it providential; that right before her eyes was the answer she was looking for. Sitting across the table from her were two sheikhs, one with a large brown warty mole on his nose and the other with an identical mole floating in his dessert. She watched mesmerised as the warty mole was scooped up with ice cream and deposited into the open eager mouth of the man opposite. She had identified her target. The man opposite, the sheikh without the mole and chewing on something hard, was the double.

Dessert marked the end of the Versailles dinner and the waiting staff undid their corsets, massaged their aching feet and waited eagerly for a signal that the night was over.

Halfhearted farewells were exchanged all round and passengers streamed out of the dining room in pairs like animals out of the Ark.

Sheikh Hasim circumvented the captain's table and with some certain malice and without the grace of a 'pardon me' issued Goldfarb the dreaded ultimatum, 'Noon in the casino tomorrow' then swished out without a backward glance followed by Sebastian and the pair of wellness lecturers close on his heels.

Like many rich spoilt men the sheikh was prone to tantrums and like most couples that live in close proximity Sebastian could tell by his demeanour, by the way he ground his teeth and squinted, that trouble was brewing. 'Is there something wrong?' he asked and while waiting for the answer, winced.

'Wrong?' The word blasted from beneath the sheikh's kaffiyah. 'Wrong?' Again he blasted. 'Not only was a filthy pig in dress-ups on my table, but because some lunatic wants to kill me over some stupid sheep I need to travel with you.'

He spat as he talked and Sebastian took a step back to avoid the spray.

'I thought I would enjoy the peace leaving my wives at home, that you would do all the small talk at the table to free me from talking to those idiots but you have nothing to say. You do not light my cigarettes as my wives would, you wear absurd underpants, and your socks smell. And the thought of having you in my bed is totally repugnant. Never will I travel with you again.'

And as an afterthought he added, 'And I am sick of having to look at myself even when I am not shaving.'

Sheikh Hasim stopped to get his breath and at that moment it came to him like a voice from a burning bush that this klutz, this clone who now stood opposite, was of his own creation. A clone in his own image but, he asked himself, what copy can ever compare to the original? This klutz did not have his god-like qualities. He must keep in mind that this idiot was created in his image for one reason only, to dodge bullets meant for him. Suddenly he felt magnanimous towards this copy of himself as one would towards a fake Rolex.

He continued in a gentler fashion, 'Perhaps we should take a little break from each other. Go and sleep on the top deck. It is a pleasant night. I am sure I will be safe alone in our cabin, and if someone is out to get me then they will find you first, so it will be all right.' With a swirl of his white robes he stalked off to his cabin.

Unless you are A-listed, acting is a precarious profession. Actors must get used to disappointments. A show is dropped by networks when ratings fall, film footage can easily end up on the cutting room floor, one may audition a dozen times and not get offered a part. Acting is not for the faint-hearted. One must sell one's soul for an acting credit or bed an ugly casting director.

All this Sebastian was willing to accept but never had he sacrificed his looks for a part on a permanent basis. He had played Quasimodo, transformed by make-up, he had worn an extra head playing an alien, he had walked on his knees in *Moulin Rouge,* but none of these changes were permanent.

If just before his fortieth birthday the writers of his sitcom hadn't killed off his character and made him feel so vulnerable he would never have answered the advertisement, he would never have considered having plastic surgery and exchanging his good looks for a bulbous nose with a wart, a pair of puffy cheeks and a moustache like Groucho. As he was now he was totally type cast, type cast to play the Sheikh forever and all for job security. What a joke, some job security! He could tell his days were numbered.

The woman with the food chain was his only chance, the American he had artfully dodged at the captain's table. If he had to play the sheikh long term then it had to be with her. These thoughts passed through his mind like tickertape as he listened to the sheikh's tirade. On and on and ending with, 'And if somebody is out to get me then they will find you first, so it will be all right.'

He watched the sheikh disappear down the corridor towards their cabin, white robes swirling. Now was his chance to get the American alone, his chance to safely pursue the deception and convince her the sheikh was his double. He saw himself winging off to America as the genuine article, houseguest of the wealthy lady and from there he would pursue the role in earnest. It was obvious to one and all that Mrs Pamela Lawson-Groves III was fishing for a husband so he could only hope that she would assume she had reeled in a really big catch.

But Pamela Lawson-Groves III seemed to have disappeared. Sebastian searched all the bars, looked in on the casino and walked every deck until finally he arrived outside her cabin door and knocked. Still no answer and with only tomorrow to seal this deal Sebastian was feeling anxious. He scribbled a note on an envelope suggesting they meet for breakfast at some outlandish hour, well before Sheikh Hasim would wake, and slid it under her cabin door. Out of ideas as to where she was he returned to his cabin to find a Do Not Disturb Sign on the door and his pajamas neatly stacked outside with a card on which was scribbled. 'Sleep tight.'

Left with no option but to sleep elsewhere he set out for the upper deck but found Major Barbara Cock blocking his way to make small talk about the Versailles dinner. She leaned in a little too close for comfort in an invasion of his private space to comment about his pajamas and make some remark about being something of a boy scout when he mentioned sleeping up on deck.

It was the longest conversation Sebastian and Major Barbara had shared since boarding and Sebastian thanked his lucky stars for his ability to mimic the sheikh. He sighed aloud when Major Barbara finally left only to be confronted by a second person on the stairs to the lido deck, a slight figure in a hoodie, face obscured, a rolled mat clutched under their arm.

'How is it up there?' Sebastian queried. The figure, head lowered, mumbled something that Sebastian failed to grasp and gave a thumb's up sign before hurrying away.

36

A Burger With The Lot

Dirk von Klimt took his meal in his cabin. There was no way on earth or sea he would involve himself in a Versailles dinner. He scanned the room service menu and decided on a burger with the lot, silently rejoicing that his fellow passengers were otherwise occupied.

The knock on his cabin door was therefore totally unexpected. It was a gentle knock and not insistent but, as he hadn't yet ordered it couldn't be room service.

He placed the painting of a tree by Japanese master Hishimongo on to the bubble wrap in readiness for transportation. Where and how, he wondered, would this exquisite painting hang? Not for a moment could he imagine the accountant known as Maurice having the space and lighting or the taste to do it justice.

Like most who sell their souls out to the devil, the devil being money made on the backs of impoverished native artists and a greedy art market, Dirk saw himself as pure as driven snow, a purist who held copies in contempt and worshipped great art. Each year on his vacation he would tour the galleries, salivate at paintings in Le Louvre, delight at the impressionists in Musée D'Orsay, spend hours with the moderns at the Guggenheim and every now and again would, by curating a genuine collection, get in touch with his true self.

But these were fleeting moments and here on board the *Pacific Belle* the devil was in command. As he reflected on the morbid fate of this prized piece while consoling himself that he was about to become considerably richer there was another knock on the cabin door. Dirk was left with no choice but to answer.

Out in the corridor leaning on a Zimmer frame stood accountant Maurice, peering up at Dirk through metal framed glasses. A badly fitting tuxedo hung awkwardly on the old man like a suit on a scarecrow and around his scrawny neck a carnival mask dangled. Dirk assumed he had left the dinner early.

'I would like to collect my painting,' Maurice wheezed, like a badly tuned Wurlitzer.

There seemed no other option but for Dirk to invite him in while trying to maintain some dignity when caught wearing Gucci pajamas. Maurice followed his

Zimmer frame into the cabin and glanced about at the forest of paintings stacked and ready for delivery.

'I'm packing. Cases go out at midnight,' Maurice wheezed, 'so I'd like to collect my painting now.'

Money was a subject Dirk avoided off the auction podium but the boldness of Maurice's request left him with no option.

'Payment usually comes before collection,' he countered.

The old man seemed prepared for this response. 'Here is my personal cheque, but if you would rather I charge it, the purser's office has my card details on file.'

Later Dirk would blame hunger for making his decision; his need to order before room service closed coupled with a quick calculation of credit card charges. Most of his clients paid for their purchase through the ship's purser. Credit card details were always kept on file. It was his usual mode of doing business. But avoiding credit card charges on a hundred thousand dollars was not to be sneezed at. If Dirk was any judge of character this old accountant from the UK was as safe as the Bank of England.

With a magnanimous flourish he handed the painting, neatly wrapped in bubble wrap to Maurice, took the cheque and smiled. 'You have done well,' he crooned. 'The provenance is on the back.'

'Yes, I think I have,' wheezed Maurice and without further ceremony he followed his Zimmer out of the cabin with the small painting clutched under his arm.

Dirk, his grey hair free flowing, reached for the phone to order his burger and wondered if the old man even knew what the provenance of a painting stood for.

37

The One That Got Away

The albatross woke early to the sound of grunting. From his perch above the lido deck the bird glanced casually down to the source of the sound. Below him, stretched out on a deck chair was a pile of white linen, crumpled and rather soiled from which peeped a toe through a hole in a sock. A hint of pink was visible to the bird's sharp eye at one end of the bundle but something black and wavy stood out against the pink much like a sea worm against the ocean blue. The bird was well fed, a gourmand in its way, but like a true sophisticate he had the occasional hankering for basics, much like chef enjoyed the occasional baked beans on toast. So it flapped its massive wings and with a 'caw' of enthusiasm took a dive down to snatch the delicious morsel, a morsel that reminded it of fishing from the sea.

Sebastian, well worse for wear from sleeping on a deckchair, had with the dawn's first light dreamt of nestling between the breasts of the American while learning the combination of her safe. Suddenly something grey and feathered belly-landed on his chest and a long black beak pecked at his moustache. It was not the lover Sebastian had been dreaming of. It is still not clear to this day which of the duo was the more alarmed. Discovering that the black and wavy morsel was not a sea worm, the albatross beat its wings, deposited some droppings out of fright and headed heavenward leaving Sebastian in a state of shock and in a soiled garment.

For most of the night Sebastian had been searching for answers as to how he could escape from his current situation. The more he searched the clearer it seemed that there was only one logical answer. The plan was diabolical but Sebastian had played the role many times before in more than one detective series. If he could pull this off then he believed his future would be secure, or at least he hoped it would be. If he were to do it then he must do it now. He must return to his cabin before his appointment to meet with Pamela Lawson-Groves III.

The lady in question had also spent a sleepless night anxiously waiting for the dawn. The scribbled note she found under her door when she got out of the bathroom held a promise of greater things to come and her mind played games with the endless possibilities. So as dawn broke over the *Pacific Belle* steaming gracefully towards her destination, an actor pretending to be a sheikh with a hole in his sock and dressed in a white garment soiled by a disappointed albatross hurried towards his cabin before a rendezvous with a thrice-widowed heiress with romantic notions who was looking for love.

And as the thrice-widowed heiress with romantic notions prepared for her meeting with a sheikh a thickset assassin and part-time psychiatrist with an honourable military background made her way towards the galley with the same romantic notions.

* * *

Sebastian crept silently into the cabin. As he had expected Sheikh Hasim lay on his back, his iPad nestled on his belly and a padded headset on his ears. Some may drink hot cocoa to lull them to sleep but Sheikh Hasim watched porn.

Sebastian padded cautiously past the sleeping sheikh. In their shared bathroom he removed the stained thawb and headdress and cast them on the dirty laundry pile. He must be naked to the waist; that was how he had played this role before. He removed his sandals and placed them neatly in the corner. Wearing only a pair of Batman underpants he shuffled over to his own bed in the adjoining room. He lifted two pillows from his bed and cradled them to his chest then tiptoed back to where the sheikh was sleeping.

Had he been more alert and less absorbed in playing his role he may have wondered why Sheikh Hasim was not blowing bubbles, a characteristic of the sheikh's when sleeping deeply. But this was life or death for Sebastian and it was all he could do to carry it through. He lunged forward throwing his weight behind the two cushions. As he fell across the face of Sheikh Hasim, he braced himself for a struggle. As the director on the detective show had taught him, he had the advantage of position.

He lay over the sheikh for some time before it occurred to him that he wasn't putting up a fight. He moved over slightly and was suddenly shocked to hear the loud and anguished bleating of sheep. He turned his head slightly and saw the screen of the computer where moving body parts usually appeared. His sudden movement dislodged the headset from the computer and flooded the room with sound. On the screen appeared the horrific sight of thousands of sheep crammed into a small airless space so close together that they could not move. They were inside what appeared to be the hold of a ship, their eyes wide with terror. Some appeared to be dead but had nowhere to fall.

It was a sight so ghastly that Sebastian had to look away. Cautiously he lifted himself off the sheikh and removed the pillows. The sheikh remained on his back, eyes closed and mouth open. Could he simply be asleep?

A deep sleep it was, one from which the sheikh seemed unlikely to return. Sebastian had played dead many times. He had even played the mummy in a Sci Fi epic so was first to admit that if playing dead was the sheikh's intention his performance could win him an Emmy.

Sebastian rummaged through his past roles until he found detective and, following the prompts, held a mirror up to the sheikh's mouth. Not the faintest sign of breathing clouded the image of the lips reflected there. Sebastian put an ear close to the open mouth but neither felt nor heard any breath. There was no pulse. The sheikh's carotid artery was flatter than a week-old bottle of beer.

Sebastian sat down on the bed beside the lifeless body. He had done it; he had killed the sheikh. This meant he could now take his place. If he could get away with it, now was the time to try. He examined his feelings and to his surprise felt nothing.

Don't touch the body, he reminded himself. He slipped a Do Not Disturb sign on the cabin door and went to work to the sound of bleating sheep. He'd seen it done before on Netflix. The passports, credit cards, cards and airline tickets were in the cabin safe. He'd memorised the code from watching Sheikh Hasim, and even knew the code for the credit cards and could forge the sheikh's signature.

Having pocketed the contents he relocked the safe. It was only when he was on his way to breakfast, dressed in a fresh thawb and keffiyeh, that it occurred to him how easy it had been to kill the sheikh, it was almost as though the sheikh had taken it lying down, or someone had been there before him.

Meeting up with Pamela Lawson-Groves III was everything Sebastian had imagined and more. Unrestricted by time and place he did his best to impersonate an eager suitor. *Of course he would be only too happy to take a look around her home in Washington, he wouldn't even mind an extended holiday to see all her properties, but only if she had the time – and no, he would be travelling with her alone, his double had personal business elsewhere.*

So it was decided that Mrs Pamela Lawson-Groves would arrange for a ticket for the sheikh to accompany her on her flight home and his luggage would follow.

Sometime mid-morning Sebastian put a call into the ship's doctor complaining that he was unable to wake his cabin companion, his double a certain Sebastian Oliver. When the doctor arrived minutes later Sebastian explained, 'He complained of chest pains after the dinner poor man, so I left him alone and slept up on deck to give him a peaceful night, I didn't wish to disturb him when I came back to change, since then I have been in the company of a fellow passenger, Mrs Pamela Lawson-Groves.'

The sheikh lay motionless on the bed, unperturbed by the loud bleating of sheep coming from an iPad balanced on his stomach and a headset dangling by a chord beside the bed, uninterested in anything going on about him.

Rather than remove the body, the doctor requested that it stay in state in the cabin until after the ship was docked late that afternoon at which time would Sebastian agree to make some burial arrangements and notify the next of kin? He readily agreed to do so.

Rather sooner than later Sebastian took the plunge and called Habibi and in his best impersonation of the sheikh brought him up to date, explaining that his double, the actor known as Sebastian, had suddenly passed away.

Although he was Sheikh Hasim's chief financial advisor, Habib Habibi was also a self-interested man. When he heard the sheikh's double had died he heaved a sigh of relief. Part of his newfound good fortune from working for the sheikh had been to link up with Blanche, the nail technician from Manchester with an hourglass figure and legs up to her armpits. Although she had fallen hard for Sebastian in the early days of his transformation, as time passed her passion for the English actor faded and if it weren't for the three carat diamond earrings she wanted for her birthday her affair with the actor may forever have remained a secret.

Remember dear reader that the three-carat diamonds, one to each ear, were the catalyst for Blanche's change of heart? As simple a girl as Blanche appeared, she knew on what side her bread was buttered. Small, round Pakistanis were not thick on the ground, particularly those who held her in esteem.

So it was that as she admired the glittering gems nestled in their bed of satin and gratefully hugged Habibi she felt a pang of conscience about her deception and decided on the spot to come clean about the acrylic mole she had modelled for the double and her time between the sheets with him.

For his part, Habibi decided not to pursue Blanche's motives but remained aware that strong physical attractions could often recur. One less competitor for the hand of his darling Blanche was something to celebrate.

* * *

Goldfarb took no delight in keeping his appointment to play blackjack with the sheikh but realised it was inevitable. The tone he had used the previous evening indicated that the shiekh was deadly serious. The voice of Goldfarb's late mother Minchal had reached fever pitch inside his head spouting warnings about him losing the winnings he had managed to acquire. *Go hide in the cabin then sneak off the ship you putz. He can afford to lose oil wells, she rasped.*

But Goldfarb could see no way out. Deep down he felt he owed the sheikh and it seemed the feeling was reciprocated. The sheikh wanted to win back his money and Goldfarb felt he owed him for stealing one of his wives on a previous voyage. A confrontation seemed inevitable no matter what his mother had to say; it came down to a matter of honour.

The casino felt like a debutante after the ball, deflated and wanting to take off her shoes. The cockney croupier, eager to go home on shore leave, threw a withering glance at Goldfarb. Goldfarb ordered a coffee and waited, and waited. He waited from noon until it was time to pack up his belongings and leave but there was no sign of Sheikh Hasim, his double or a wife. For all intents and purposes it seemed all bets were off. *Be thankful you klutz,* his mother's voice echoed, and thankful he was.

Back in his cabin the butler, hand outstretched waiting for a gratuity and cracked a phony smile. With less than twenty-four hours until the next bunch came on board he had lots to do.

Ships must follow unique itineraries on a never-ending route to exotic destinations. No matter what disaster may happen at sea, a cruise ship is programmed to keep to a schedule. Port visits are planned to take on board passengers, while other passengers were due to disembark. Life on board the cruise ship is planned down to the minute, Joggers would circumvent the deck, runners ran to nowhere on machines, and breakfast would always be served in the salon from eight.

As Goldfarb stood in line to disembark, he was asked to stand aside as two medics carrying Sheikh Hasim in a green body bag stepped past him down the gangway. He watched as they hastily slid the bagged body through the open doors of a waiting hearse. Goldfarb hadn't socialised that much. On a ship that carried more than a thousand passengers it was difficult to meet everyone on board. He wondered who it could be in that body bag. He paused to reflect and found the moment sobering. A quote from Woody Allen came to mind about *not being afraid of dying as long as you weren't there when it happened. Yes.* He reflected *the whole thing was a numbers game and some poor shmuck's number just came up.* His mood shifted as he detected Brenda's mane of red hair in the waiting crowd.

It was good to be home.

Brenda had sent Goldfarb a text advising him she would be waiting dockside when the ship berthed. He couldn't wait to hug her. A week was far too long to be apart from the woman he loved. But it had been worth it. Brenda had already found them an apartment in a half empty building and with the money they had both made playing blackjack they could easily pay out the lease on their old one and escape from the dreadful pimply rock musician. Maybe he would see if Brenda fancied learning bridge or maybe that was not such a good idea.

A waft of Patchouli eau de toilette from a passing blonde, Brenda's favourite fragrance, transported Goldfarb back to how he and she had met and to wonder yet again about what happened to Sheikh Hasim. He mentally found himself back in the ship's casino at that very moment when Goldfarb and the Sheikh had first met and seen the woman in red seated at the blackjack table. Goldfarb grinned as he remembered how the Sheikh couldn't recognise his wife without a burqa. The shmuck of a Sheikh was competing for his own wife and obviously considered no better way to win over an opponent than to befriend him, so he had leaned past the woman in red to address Goldfarb. Goldfarb remembered every word.

'It appears that we have the same sexual object in mind.' The Sheik had salaamed and tweaked his puce lips at Goldfarb in a friendly fashion. But Sheik Hasim did not factor Goldfarb's late mother Minchal into the equation. She was no shrinking violet. When Minchal spoke, the earth shook, and her husband or partner of the moment trembled. Minchal came from a long line of liberated females who believed that it was the woman who fashioned a family out of the clay of the provider, that within a family a woman's voice was equal to any man. So, spearheaded by the conditioning of his Jewish mother, Goldfarb had placed a hand upon the white-frocked chest of Sheik Hasim and shoved him backwards with the words, "I believe you are blocking this lady's view, and your tone is insulting." This simple line of dialogue melted any doubts that Brenda Willing may have had about the inscrutable Goldfarb. Like two moths attracted to the same flame, they hesitated, eyes and hands glued together in some eternal bondage. Not known for wasting any time on lost causes Sheikh Hasim had gathered up his thawb and headed for the door.

From that moment a warm sensation had crept through Goldfarb and nestled like a dove within his solar plexus and he knew without a doubt he was on a winning streak. Robbed of his usual temerity, he had grabbed the pile of chips his newfound love had left behind her as she sashayed out of the casino and slammed a portion on the table. He was bonded. Now he played for two. Her abandoned chips were now his responsibility. Like children waiting to be nourished, he would nurture them and watch them grow, and when he met the woman in red the following evening he would not come empty handed. He had her winnings with him. And so it was that as he inhaled a familiar perfume and followed a zipped green body bag down a ramp and off the *Pacific Belle* history was repeating itself. He had Brenda's winnings with him, winnings that would free them forever from a frightful din.

He later told her, after she had greeted him on dockside, that she would never guess who had been on board, who he had come face to face with at the Captains table. None other, he explained, than her previous common law husband Sheikh Hasim who actually failed to recognize him and even failed to keep a rendezvous with Goldfarb for a return match at the Casino, a match that Goldfarb thought inevitable. Judging by the tone the Sheikh had used the previous evening Goldfarb knew he meant business and was deadly serious about recouping some of his losses. So it was astonishing, Goldfarb explained, that although Goldfarb waiting long after the appointed time Sheikh Hasim failed to appear. While Goldfarb waxed lyrical about this surprise encounter, Brenda did what wives have always done in similar situations, she tuned out and thought about her shopping list. As she turned the key in the lock of their new apartment she caught his final words and smiled as he described how the Sheikh now travelled with a double and did not bring his wives along. *Four wives with a week to plan revenge for being left behind. Heaven help Hasim when he gets home, she thought.*

She pushed open the heavy aged oak doors to the apartment and triumphantly announced 'No neighbours!' The apartment was large and airy and opened out onto a small paved courtyard under a canopy of vines. A table was set up in the courtyard with two champagne flutes and a magnum sweating in an ice bucket. *This road goes to nowhere so very little traffic passes* Brenda hastened to assure him. Their road wound back up the hill and out of sight, and from where they were wound down into the small yacht harbour. Goldfarb sank into a canvas chair, glanced upward to the clear blue sky glimmering through the vines and silently gave thanks to his mother Minchal, and any other powers that be, for granting them a life of peace and quiet. Brenda filled their flutes from the magnum and they toasted each other in silence.

Further up the hill and around a bend a group of Hare Krishna in saffron robes, each with a forehead smeared with red and clutching tambourines, trumpets, flutes and drums, assembled outside a temple, behind a leader head shaved but for a single pigtail, who raised his drumsticks and beat a drumroll to signal the procession was about to begin. Thus rallied the colourful disciples formed a line and, trumpets blasting, bells jangling and drums rolling they wove and clanged their way down the road and around the bend on their thrice daily ritual toward the boat harbour, past an old grey building with a heavy aged oak door where a canopy of vines umbrella'd over a courtyard, and where two lovers were celebrating their hard-earned sound of silence over a flute of champagne.

38

A Squirt of Opium Eau de Parfum

The albatross was old. He had followed the great ones, the *Queens Mary* and *Elizabeth* on Transatlantic crossings. He was barely more than a chick when he discovered it was easier to live off ships than nosedive into the ocean for his dinner. His heart skipped a beat whenever he spotted a white-frocked chef on deck. They were his favourite people. But the great *Queens* had been taken to dry dock to be renamed and renewed and during this hiatus he discovered the sea-going yachts and smaller vessels all with Master Chefs on board.

If he were to grade the food on board this cruise from one to ten he would have to give it nine. He watched the chef with the egghead and the ears like clamshells mount the steps onto the top deck and release a stream of inhaled smoke up into the clear blue sky. The albatross felt fondly of him. He had enjoyed this Chef's Halibut in Hollandaise; he sensed purity about this chef's cuisine. His little heart ached with gratitude. He felt in awe of this chef 's culinary skills. The man was a master, a true master.

One small round black eye swivelled to follow a steward and watched as the man polished the brass handrail with the sleeve of his white uniform. The bird took note that he polished it with care. A change of position was necessary the bird decided.

The albatross soared and lingered in the air, white and shimmering then he glided silently to a handrail on the upper deck. The chef had gone below. The bird took careful aim. The acid of his missile would eat into the polished surface, experience taught him so. He stretched his neck and strained as he positioned his rear end over the handrail his huge wings corseting his well-fed body. Swivelling his small head backwards he watched as a green and white and chalky globule dropped through the air and landed on the handrail below, onto the brass. It was a direct hit.

* * *

Chef Armand had ridden high after the dinner, high on the look of horror displayed by the sheikhs when confronted by a hog's head tablepiece; high on the amount of *crème fraîche*, the butter and lard and rich sauces those bone thin, weight obsessed gym junkies had no choice but to consume, high on the look of contempt on the face of the lecturers who would turn back the clock to the stone age and have us all eating berries and leaves.

Yes, he had ridden high on the Versailles dinner but came down with a thump when he read the captain's note. A more resilient man could count his blessings and rejoice at the chance of leave with pay and, had it been his own idea, it was something he could accept. But Chef Armand was a man of thin skin and inflated ego and such men tend to wallow. And wallow chef did as, with head low and shoulders drooped, he led his small pig Arafat back into the galley, not to prepare the menu for the passengers about to board the ship on the next leg of the cruise but to make preparations for his last day on board.

Mahmud was ready with a bowl of food for Arafat, chef's brew of coffee and a *Crème Brûlée*, but chef did not return his greeting and continued to his office feet dragging.

After creating a masterpiece, a dinner that had never been done on board ship before, having been heaped with praise and toasted in champagne by a grateful captain, he had then been asked to leave the ship. Not in person but via a note. At first, he thought it was a practical joke but closer examination of the piece of paper revealed a signature, the spidery signature of Captain Svensen. *Take three months long service starting from tomorrow by order of management. Further contracting to be reviewed in three months. Please note: Live pigs are not allowed to live on board.*

And as t*he Pacific Belle* struggled against her moorings as a racehorse would against a tether the ship's executive chef reflected on the state of his affairs and pondered on the injustices of the world. And as chef contemplated suicide while sampling Mahmud's *crème brûlée* the ship's remaining passengers collected their belongs and prepared to disembark, some eager to escape, some not.

Deep within the hull of the ship, a woman of military bearing packed her few possessions inside a weathered leather duffel bag, a duffel bag that was her hearth and home and quietly examined all her options. Further cruising holidays were definitely not for her, yet somehow she did not want to leave this ship. Even though she felt a certain satisfaction at a job well done and could anticipate a hefty bonus something did not feel quite right. She took a few moments to fill in a time sheet for the man on the island married to a dog, and paused to review her own uncertain future. It suddenly occurred to her she had nothing planned at all, that the void around her solar plexus certainly wasn't hunger. Could it simply be a sign of emptiness? She signed off on her time sheet and without hesitation aimed a generous squirt of Opium *Eau de Parfum* behind each ear. Then she picked up her duffel bag and headed for the galley, her defences lowered and her expectations high.

39

Smoke and Mirrors

Bereft of passengers the ship resembled an amusement park at closing time with litter left by a thousand guests homeward bound, luggage bulging. The atmosphere on board had lightened now that the passengers had disembarked. Deck crew stood around in groups and smoked while cabin crew, the butlers and the maids tackled the making up of cabins and the cleaning of the public spaces in readiness to take on another batch of passengers the following morning.

And earlier as Sheikh Hasim tucked away secure within a moss green body bag and unaware of bumps and grinds, content in his dreamless sleep, free from nagging wives, from doubles, from the ghosts of an unhappy childhood and from dodging drying cabinets, was trundled down toward a sun-filled exit his cabin butler, a highly superstitious native of the Philippines named Sanchez, mumbled incantations and sprinkled the cabin with a mysterious dust to ward off evil spirits. A death at sea was not unusual.

The final day of a short cruise was the busiest for Dirk von Klimt. Larger paintings were packaged and made ready for transport. Rarely did he emerge from his cabin until the ship was docked. By then the passengers had settled all accounts and it was time for him to transact business.

The purser, an Australian, ran a pen down the list Dirk von Klimt had given him checking out the cabin numbers. 'Something wrong here, mate, no one named Maurice Smart from the UK on this passenger list.'

'Cabin 240,' Dirk repeated, pointing to the name on the list and the cabin number beside it. "Woman from Greece named Katzizis in cabin 240. You sure you got the name right?'

Dirk von Klimt turned a bright shade of purple. 'An old guy on a Zimmer frame, he could hardly walk.' The truth began to dawn on him that he might be a victim of fraud. 'Do you have his credit card details?'

'Mate, if he isn't listed as being on board how can I have his credit card details?'

'Let me run through the ID photographs you took when passengers came on board, don't they need to swipe a card to get on and off?' Dirk asked as a last resort.

The purser handed him the proof sheet but the image of Maurice Smart the accountant from the UK, the man with the Zimmer was nowhere to be seen.

'Go through the list of who paid a single cabin supplement, he has to be somewhere, he bought a painting from me,' Dirk insisted.

'Oh, mate; we did away with the single supplement on short trips long ago, too many complaints from widows. Sorry, mate, looks as though you've been had.'

Later that evening when the cleaning of the *Pacific Belle* was complete a folded Zimmer frame, discovered in the casino and left behind on disembarkation, was brought up to lost property.

The following day, back in the UK, a train pulled into a rural station where a black Mercedes was waiting.

The driver turned and smiled. 'Did you have a good holiday? He was a man of wide girth and wider smile, a mainstay of the college, the master, a wiry man in his late sixties, nodded and smiled back. It was good to be home.

The car passed along the English hedgerows to the iron gates of the college. Beyond, a drive bordered by oaks meandered up to the beginning of the quadrangle and beyond that the towers of the school were visible. The master, Cyril Montague, could see that in the weeks he had been away the spring flowers had begun to bloom. The gates opened automatically and the school limousine cruised up the drive and deposited the master and his luggage at the door of School House. Not that there was much luggage; the master travelled light, a carry-on hanging bag and a small parcel wrapped in bubble wrap.

He loved the college and teaching his favourite subjects of mathematics and art history. This term he would concentrate on getting the cricket team up to scratch. He dumped his things inside the small apartment in the century-old Tudor building. It was good to feel earth beneath his feet again.

Eager to stretch his legs after a long air and train journey, the master pulled on a tracksuit, grabbed a mat and headed for the lawns beside the lake, his favourite spot for doing press-ups and squats. Several of the boys were waiting for him, his favourites, the year nines, young enough to know what they are doing but adventurous enough to break the rules.

'Do one for us, sir, do one of your tricks,' they chorused and from the pocket of his tracksuit he drew a pack of cards. He was good at sleight of hand.

The group of boys, pimply and eager, threw out the question, one that they always asked this teacher, 'How do you do that, sir?

'All smoke and mirrors lads, just smoke and mirrors.'

And as he carried out his one hundred press-ups, a habit he engaged in daily no matter where he was, he added this advice, 'Generally people believe what they see, and they rarely look below the surface.'

No one on board the *Pacific Belle* had looked below the surface at the old man with the Zimmer frame; he was of no interest to anyone. A teacher's salary was pretty basic and years ago Cyril had found a way to take the occasional holiday to indulge in a little luxury he could not otherwise afford and very occasionally, by foul means or fair, he would acquire a painting for his small art collection. His late father was an art curator who put together collections for rich and famous people. But being scrupulously honest and therefore poor he never did manage to put a collection of his own together.

A colleague passed him on the lawn as he did his push-ups and yelled.

"Would you care for a rubber of bridge after dinner, Cyril?

'Have you ever tried blackjack,' Cyril yelled after him. 'It's quite an interesting game.'

Tomorrow, term started but before then Cyril had a task to complete, to unpack a small painting by the Japanese artist Hishimongo and add it to his diminutive but exquisite art collection. He knew his students would find it interesting.

40

Gentleman's Agreement

It has been said that no silk purse has ever been made from a sow's ear but Sebastian the actor, now living as the Sheikh Hasim, seemed to be an exception. Although to the outside world his outer countenance appeared unchanged the same could not be said of his behavior.

Speculation abounded among his close associates about the possible use of drugs, and there were questions asked about the state of his mental condition. Whatever the reasons, Sheikh Hasim had returned to the Emirates following an extended holiday in the USA an utterly different man. To all intents and purposes his experience in the USA had caused radical changes.

It was generally acknowledged that these changes were certainly for the better. He smiled more and sulked less and seemed to think more deeply. He was no longer prone to tantrums and developed a passion for daytime television. Whereas previously the sheikh had avoided business dealings, the first decision he made on his return was to close down his chain of shawarma restaurants and ban the importing of any livestock, be it sheep or other forms, by any of his businesses. And in a move that surprised everyone he commissioned a study on the possible irrigation of the desert.

He rarely spoke Arabic these days saying he now preferred to converse in English and as a symbol of his attitude to the emancipation of the modern woman he presented each of his wives with a gold Mercedes on condition that they take driving lessons.

Every few months he headed for the USA and it was said that there he had a mistress, a blonde woman of means who introduced him to Mormons in Salt Lake City, rodeos in Texas, politicians in Washington DC, and southern fried chicken. There was talk among the elders that the sheikh's values had been violated by his time in the USA with this decadent western woman.

Habibi, who was the most affected by the changes in the sheikh, accepted them wordlessly. But every now and then, when his mistress Blanche applied pressures on him for a new house or other expensive gifts, he would casually introduce the subject of a warty mole or the limitations of body art when in conversation over a morning coffee or a business lunch with the sheikh.

And at such times a look would pass between the men, a gentlemen's agreement, and another zero would be added to Habib Habibi's pay cheque.

41

L'oreille du Cochon
(The Ear Of The Pig)

Chef Armand looked out through his kitchen window and his heart warmed.

Never in his fifty years did he imagine that one day he would have a family. Almost always a seafaring man, Chef Armand had at last come to ground.

Beyond the window of his cottage loomed his truffle orchard of oak trees and in the distance in the neighboring field recently acquired from his neighbours, was a field of lavender in bloom. The colour of the lavender blazing vivid in the sunlight moved chef to creativity. Today he would prepare a *Pear Tarte Tatin*, he decided. His restaurant, *L'oreille du Cochon* that roughly translates to The Ear Of The

Pig, had been up and running for more than a year and a food writer from Paris had indicated he would be paying the restaurant a visit very soon. Maybe he would pick up a Michelin star or two, maybe even three, he speculated.

Memory is a remarkable thing. All the frustrations that had found a home with Chef Armand had disappeared miraculously. Patrons who frequented his restaurant, and they came from far and wide, did so because they loved his food. But when it comes to running a business there must always be a profit and as much as chef avoided compromise the blurb on the back of his menu showed his attitudes had softened. After all, he had a truffle orchard and a restaurant to run and a mortgage to pay. So across the back of his menu in letters bold he had listed the health benefits of truffles, that they are low in fat, that they are a source of carbs, that they are cholesterol free and, in a footnote that came with a disclaimer, he added that some say truffles are said to be an aphrodisiac.

As he viewed the field of lavender there appeared a figure in a large straw hat carrying a basket. Trotting along beside her was what appeared to be a dog led on the leash by a boy.

Chef waved and she waved back. It was his Barbara, gathering lavender to put on the tables, the lavender that filled the dining room with freshness. With her was young Mahmoud, his *sous chef*, who rarely left her side when he was not cooking. And that was no dog but Arafat, larger now, fatter now, but still the loving and affectionate truffle pig trotting along at their heels through the field of lavender.

Barbara had in part come clean about her previous life, that of a major in the US army, and they had both laughed about her posing as a food writer at the request of the ship's captain.

Chef remembered well when first he arrived back from sea, Arafat by his side and the threatening glances and comments thrown out at him by his enemy the imam. A fiercer enemy now that chef housed the imam's nephew, Mahmoud, under his roof. For the first few months chef kept his truffle pig and Mahmoud well out of reach of the imam but that all changed when Barbara came to stay.

On that awful day, when chef was asked to leave the ship, dismissed as executive chef by the captain in a handwritten note delivered to his cabin by a junior officer, when he felt like a jilted lover, unappreciated and cast aside, that the world at large had let him down, it was then that Major Barbara Cock, armed with a dose of common sense, had come to his rescue.

It was Barbara who made him realise that this was a blessing in disguise, that three months of leave with pay was the ideal opportunity to start out on his own.

Yes, she would come to visit as soon as her own affairs were put in order and it was she who suggested that making Mahmoud part of his team would be a good idea.

True to her word, Barbara arrived at his cottage one month later. By then the frenzied imam was sending threatening letters demanding the return of his nephew Mahmoud and it seemed from the number of calls to prayer that happened over every twenty-four hours that the imam had increased them by at least two.

Strangely enough with Barbara's arrival in the province chef's luck took a turn for the better. Within a month, the imam suffered a fatal heart attack and died. It was about this time that Barbara, with her army rank of major and experience in negotiating, did a deal with the imam's widow to rebuild the mosque closer to a larger town in return for the land on which it stood. Local businesses and a neighboring music school contributed to the cost. The wife of the imam, Mahmoud's aunt, and a reasonable woman prevented from having a voice while her husband was alive, gladly accepted the major's offer and made peace with her nephew Mahmoud.

The land on which the mosque once stood was now their field of lavender.

Every few months Barbara would be called away on business that she never discussed with Armand, but it was unspoken between them that this was now her home and Armand, Mahmoud and Arafat were family. Talk of a spring wedding was in the air.

Footnote

Mr Rufus and his canine Mrs Rufus heaped praise upon Major Barbara Cock who received a special bonus for a job well done from her client on the island. On viewing photographs of the target after she had carried out her mission Mr Rufus made the comment, 'One less asshole in the world today.'

Major Cock reported that the target was made aware of the reasons for the action, that it was a clean job and carried out without consequences. The major further guaranteed no repercussions would ensue. She enclosed her invoice and the details of her bank account and thanked the gentleman for his business.

He praised her for a job well done. She was, at the very least, professional.

L'oreille du Cochon
(The Ear Of The Pig)

A MESSAGE FROM THE CHEF

Dear Patron,

As you have dined at my restaurant you must understand cuisine so I should like to share with you some little known facts about pigs. Many religious groups consider these beautiful animals unclean. It is not for me to argue with religious groups as I am an agnostic but I must say a word or two in defence of my curly tailed pink friends.

You may have heard the famous saying by Sir Winston Churchill *"dogs look up to man; cats look down to man but pigs look us straight in the eye and see an equal".* And he was right. Pigs are *très intelligents.* They can solve simple problems. Of course they are unable to work out a *mot croisé* – a crossword but in other ways they are smart. They are, in fact as intelligent as most three year olds, and a lot cleaner. The pig is *tre`s propre* and will not soil where he sleeps but a child and some elderly people do. Neither does he sweat, as pigs have no sweat glands. So when you hear the phrase "to sweat like a pig" it is nonsense. Pigs make good pets. The pig is extremely social and – *se pelotonne dans son lit,* – they love to snuggle up. The actor and *auteur* George Clooney kept a pig as a pet at one time, or so they write in magazines. I, Chef Armand also keep a pet pig, although my pig Arafat earns her keep. So George Clooney and myself share a love for pigs. I would like to say that George and I also share a love of French food, but it seems he prefers to eat pasta.

I would like that George would come and eat at L'oreille du Cochon next time he passes by. I will feed him on the house.

Pigs communicate. They make different oinks, grunts and squeals and each sound has a meaning. When a pig is stressed his squeal can be as loud as a supersonic airliner, so my advice to everyone is, don't ever stress a pig.

The pig is revered in China. It is one of the twelve animals of the Chinese Zodiac. The Chinese believe that the pig is a sign of virility, that people born in the year of the pig are blessed with good luck and wealth.

But it is the pig's remarkable sense of smell that makes this animal unique and perfect for hunting truffles. Arafat sniffs out truffles that grow at the base of the oak trees in our orchard behind the restaurant that enables me to prepare my cuisine extraordinaire, because the flavor of the truffle is exceptional. If you wish to cook with truffle we have some for sale, along with a cookbook. You will find no finer truffle anywhere.

It has been said, although not proven that the truffle can act as an aphrodisiac, that even the smell of a truffle can as they say 'turn you on'. The great gastronome Jean-Anthelme Brillat-Savarin is quoted as saying:

'As soon as the word truffle is spoken, it awakens lustful and erotic memories among the skirt-wearing sex and erotic and lustful memories among the beard-wearing sex.'

Even the emperor Napoleon was said to have eaten truffles to increase his masculine potency.

So enjoy your meal. And afterwards, who knows!!!

Bonne Chance
Executive Chef Armand

L'oreille du cochon
Specialty Truffle Restaurant.

Truffle Cookbook

(A Work in Progress)

Gratin of Leeks with Truffles

Ingredients

- 4 tender leeks
- 80g of butter
- 30g of flour
- ½ litre of milk

- Salt and pepper
- a little bit of grated Gruyere
- 32g of truffle, grated

Preparation

Trim the leeks and keep the white and yellow part of the leeks. Wash carefully. Cut them into julienne strips, and then cook them, in butter till wilted. Make a béchamel sauce. Take a flat casserole plate, butter it and put in one layer of béchamel sauce. Put in the julienne leeks and cover with truffle morsels. Cover the rest with the béchamel. Sprinkle with grated Gruyere. Put in the oven for 10 minutes at 180 degrees.

Tournedos with Truffles

Ingredients

- 16g of grated fresh truffles
- 20cl of liquid cream
- Salt and pepper
- 4 tournedos steaks
- 250g of fresh pasta.

Preparation

Mix the cream, the grated truffles, salt and pepper and infuse for one hour before cooking in a sealed container.

Cooking

Cook the fresh pasta al dente. Pan-fry the steaks in butter. When the steaks are ready – rare to medium rare – deglaze the pan with the cream and truffle mixture, but do not let the mixture boil. Add the truffle cream to the pasta and steak. Serve immediately

Ravioilis de Royans and
Chicken Breasts with Truffles

Ingredients

- 16g of fresh truffles
- 20cl of crème fraiche
- 600g of raviolis de royans (prepared ravioli – wheat pasta filled with cheese and herbs)
- 4 chicken breasts
- Salt and pepper

Preparation

Mix the cream with the grated truffles, salt, pepper, mix and seal in a container for one hour before cooking.

Cooking

Cook the chicken breasts in a pan with butter. Boil the ravioli until cooked. Deglaze the chicken pan with the cream and truffle mixture, stirring constantly for one minute but do not bring to boil. Serve Ravioli covered with chicken and truffle cream.

Truffle Soup with Cèpes (Mushrooms) and Royans Ravioilis

Ingredients

- ½ litre of duck broth
- 200g of Porcino or any variety of mushroom
- 100g of fresh truffles
- 150g of Raviolis (wheat pasta filled with cheese and herbs)
- 40g of butter
- 2 spoons of olive oil
- Salt and pepper

Preparation

Make the duck broth using a duck carcass, 2 onions, 2 carrots and 1 bouquet garni, Cover with 2 litres water and simmer for 2 hours, then pass through a sieve, cool and remove fat.

Cooking

Cut the cepes (mushrooms) into pieces and sauté in olive oil for 3 minutes. Add the duck broth and let cook or 20 minutes. Add the butter, salt, pepper. Sauté the raviolis for one minute in good quality olive oil and add to the soup. Decorate with sliced truffles.

Truffle Omelette

Ingredients

- 5 – 6 eggs
- 16g of truffles cut into thin slices
- Salt and pepper

Preparation

Place six slices of truffle aside for decoration. One hour before serving break eggs into a bowl, add remaining truffles and seal bowl to infuse. Just before cooking season eggs with salt and pepper.

Cooking

Use a small frying pan to make 2 individual omelettes. Heat the pan with a small spoon of butter. When the butter is hot, pour in the egg and truffle mixture. Cook on high heat, stirring with wooden spatula, make a chausson (slipper) and then form the omelettes. Decorate with sliced truffles.

Brioches with Truffle Sauce Mornay

Ingredients

- 2.5 litres of milk
- 80g of butter
- 30 g of flour

- ½ box of ready made quenelles de brochet or prepare your own.

A quenelle is a mixture of creamed fish or meat, sometimes combined with breadcrumbs, with a light egg binding, formed into an egg-like shape, and then cooked. The usual preparation is by poaching, 50g of fresh truffles, 60g of grated Gruyere, 1 egg yolk, 8 brioches, salt and pepper.

Preparation

To make a béchamel sauce: melt the 50g of butter over low heat, add the flour and stir. Cook for several minutes, stirring. Add the boiling milk in small quantities and continue stirring. Cook for ten minutes over low heat. To make the Mornay, add the grated Gruyere and the egg yolk to the hot béchamel sauce.

Cooking

Keep aside 8 slices of truffles for decoration. Cut the rest in small cubes and the quenelles in slices. Mix all of this with the Mornay, adding the truffle juice and set aside 30 minutes. Scoop out the brioche Then fill them with the above mixture and put them in the oven for 10 minutes on low heat. Serve decorated with truffle slices.

Chicken Liver Parfait

Ingredients

- 250g of chicken livers
- 250g of soft butter
- 60g of truffles
- Salt and pepper
- 100ml of white wine.

Preparation

Marinate the livers in the wine and the salt and pepper for one hour. Cook the livers in a pot with the marinade stirring occasionally. When livers are pink take the pot off the fire and blend in a blender adding the butter. Cut the truffles into julienne strips. Before putting the mixture in a terrine, mix the cut truffles with the liver mixture and blend. Decorate with remaining truffles.

Soft Boiled Eggs with Truffles

Ingredients

- 4 eggs
- 40 g of butter
- 20 g of grated truffles
- Sour dough bread – preferably freshly baked.

Preparation

Place 4 eggs with the grated truffles, uncooked and in their shell, into a sealed container. Leave for 48 hours. The eggs will absorb the truffle flavour through the shell. Blend small amount of grated truffle with butter and set aside.

Cooking

Cook the eggs as you normally would for soft-boiled eggs. Butter toast with the butter blended with grated truffle. The boiled eggs will be perfumed with the truffle.

From me to you...

For those readers who are not familiar with how we came to arrive at our current food revolution – one theory is that it all began in a garden, that biblical Garden of Eden. It took just one bite of the forbidden fruit, one crunch of the flesh, one drop of heavenly apple juice to launch us on our way to the expansive world of food sensations.

A bible sceptic may choose to believe that a few hundred thousand years ago a jaded caveman put down the piece of charred meat he was gnawing on and grunted, "What can I put on this crap to give it some taste?" But it took the French to move things along when during the *Aurignacian* period a Gaul made the startling discovery that water in a gourd would bubble when held over a fire and that wrapping a piece of raw meat in leaves before throwing it into this boiling water could provide quite a tasty morsel. The current trend toward a *Paleo* diet seems to confirm that we are simply running out of new ideas.

You may think that garlic is a new culinary discovery but that is not the case. The Ancient Egyptians smothered their food in it and let it suffice to say that Cleopatra probably chewed on mint leaves before seducing Mark Anthony. But of course it was the hedonist Epicurus who picked up the gauntlet in Ancient Greece with his philosophy of Epicureanism and passed it to the citizens of the Roman Empire who really took the business of eating seriously. They replaced the simple meal with a banquet, and would eat so much that they needed to recline while eating to aid digestion. Their cooks invented countless ways to render food unrecognizable, a skill that chefs have been practicing ever since.

King Louis XIV also known as The Sun King was on the French throne from 1643 until his death in 1715. As well as being the fashion doyen of his age he was quite the gourmand. Banquets were central to his court at the palace of Versailles. His steward Louis de Béchamel invented the béchamel sauce and Louis's secret second wife Francoise d'Aubigne', Marquise de Maintenon was said to have founded a school that awarded blue ribbons to girls who won honors in cooking. (A malcontented chef named Vincent

La Chapelle waged war against Monsieur Béchamel's famous Béchamel sauce and failed. This could be seen as the early rumblings of a *Nouvelle Cuisine*)

In 1762 we got a taste of our first fast food when the English nobleman Montagu the 4th Earl of Sandwich asked, in the midst of a card game, for a serving of beef between two slices of bread that he could eat with one hand without having to leave the card table. Obviously this behavior caused quite a stir because to this day this practice has been maintained and this humble meal is still known as a *Sandwich* in memory of the Earl.

So, where did one go to experience these food sensations?

By 1765 the first basic *"Haute Cuisine"* restaurant was opened in Paris by a Frenchman named Boulanger serving only one dish, sheep's feet simmered in white sauce. Twenty years afterwards the first restaurant as we know it today opened. It was called *La Grande Taverne de Londres* and the owner was Antoine Beauvilliers (1754-1817) who became the first famous restaurateur and host. The idea caught on and by 1790s there were 100 such restaurants in Paris.

Celebrity Chefs are not thin on the ground today but their forerunner certainly was unique. Frenchman Marie-Antoine Carême was the first recorded *celebrity Chef.* He was an early practitioner and exponent of the elaborate style of cooking known as *grand cuisine*, or cuisine *classique*, the "high art" of French cooking, a grandiose style of cookery favored by both international royalty, the *nouveau riche* of Paris and of course our Chef Armand at his small and traditional restaurant *L'Oreille du Cochon*, Marseille (Google for directions – or check the Michelin guide)

Bonne Chance
Chilli Kippen. Melbourne, Australia 2020.

About the Author

CHILLI KIPPEN was born in the UK and travelled through fifty-two countries before calling Australia home. She was widely read as a features and travel writer for major magazines, including Vogue, New York Times Magazines, Penthouse, Playboy and the Hollywood Reporter before turning her hand to writing comedy.

She is an award-winning documentary filmmaker and screenwriter and has worked in Hollywood and Australia.

Her first novel – *The Captain Loves Caviar* features the debut of Pushkin Goldfarb, a professional gambler from New York and his adventure on board the 5-star cruise ship *Pacific Belle*. It is the first in a hilarious series focusing on Goldfarb's gambling and sea-going lifestyle and the bizarre world he encounters at sea and on land. *The Chef Who Made Onions Cry* is the second book in the series.

Chilli and her family divide their time between the coastal tropics of Australia and the city. They share their lives with their adored tribe of King Charles Spaniels.

 Matador